Layla

Book Three of
The Siblings O'Rifcan Series

By Katharine E. Hamilton

ISBN-13: 978-0-692-19262-7

Layla

www.katharinehamilton.com

Cover Design by Kerry Prater.

Dedicated to all my aunts.
Never underestimate the impact and love of an aunt for their nieces or nephews. Now that I am one, I somewhat understand this unique relationship even better.

Aunts are special, but I've always thought I was quite spoiled in this area.

Especially when they allow you to have a Little Mermaid birthday party at their house with a bunch of eight-year-old little girls running around screaming and splashing in the pool.

Acknowledgments

It's always hard to think of everyone who's helped shape a manuscript into an actual book. I hope I remember all of you.

My husband, Brad, is a pretty awesome guy. I thank him for loving me and tolerating an unkempt house while I finished writing this book.

My family. They are on this journey with me and have supported me every step of the way.

My alpha and beta readers. I have been a bit behind schedule this time around and they've been awesome to work with around my lollygagging.

Thanks to my editor, Lauren Hanson. She's forever patient and thorough. I appreciate you, Lauren!

And thanks to my readers. I love meeting you. I love hearing from you. And I love writing for you. You guys are awesome.

« CHAPTER ONE »

$\mathcal{A}$ *handsaw shrilled.* Hammers pounded. And the smell of sawdust clung to the air amidst the chaos that was once Chloe's flower shop. Riley and Murphy, her brothers, held the wooden frame of what would soon be a display counter as Conor McCarthy hammered it together. Tool belts, muscles, and polished smiles filled the room as man after man fluttered about the space to help transform it, not only into Chloe's flower shop but also Layla's Potions. She went with the name due to all the females of the family granting her the title of wizard when it came to her bath salts, candles, lotions, and scrubs. It was growing on her. She watched as her younger sister, Chloe, finished off a flower arrangement and set it inside one of her coolers. She wiped her hands on a towel and smiled. "What do you think, sister?"

"'Tis coming along just fine. Not bad scenery either." Layla O'Rifcan eyed a handsome man that was part of Riley's construction crew. He flashed a dazzling smile as he passed by and she returned it. Naturally.

Chloe shook her head. "Aye, I will agree with you there. If only they were here to buy flowers." She chuckled as Layla set her purse behind Chloe's counter, both sisters standing to observe the workspace transforming before them. "Will be lovely once they're done."

Layla nodded and watched as Murphy yelled from atop a ladder and ducked out of the way of a new beam being lifted into place. The bell on the door jingled and had both women turning to find Rhea and Heidi entering. Rhea Conners beamed as she spotted them, ducking her way under boards and stepping over stacks of supplies as she headed towards them. Heidi Rustler, on the other hand, made a beeline towards their brother, Riley.

"It's looking fantastic!" Rhea hugged each sister in excitement. "Looks like Riley has all hands on deck for you guys."

"Only because he needs the project finished by the end of the week so as not to lose pace on his museum work in Galway," Layla pointed out. "But handy in a pinch, that Riley." They watched as he

2

paused in his work to swoop Heidi into his arms and plant a solid kiss to her lips.

"And to think," Rhea said, "she thought she didn't love him."

The women all laughed as they turned towards a catalog on Chloe's counter top. "This is it?" Rhea asked.

"Aye." Chloe opened to a page and handed it to Rhea.

"Beautiful." The large floral arrangement was perfect for her upcoming trip to Cape Clear to visit the O'Rifcan grandparents with Claron, the youngest O'Rifcan brother. "Nanny will love it. Let's go with this one."

"And where is Clary this fine afternoon? No cows need milking at this time," Layla pointed out.

"He's harvesting this week. He feels bad he can't help with this project, but duty calls." Rhea sighed as she thought of him and the sisters rolled their eyes.

"Still in love with our brother, I see." Chloe giggled as Rhea pretended to swoon. "Though I must say Murphy's giving him a run for his money today." Rhea nodded towards the shirtless brother as he worked on hammering trim around the door frame.

"Oy." Chloe shook her head. "So many women customers today. Now I see why." She laughed as another woman entered the shop. "Let's see what excuse she has to buy flowers," Chloe whispered as she plastered a friendly smile on her face in welcome.

Layla tugged Rhea out of the way and towards the corner of the room and they watched the work continue. "Thoughts?" Layla asked her.

Rhea surveyed the space. "It's going to look wonderful. Polished. Sleek. And just the right touch of coziness."

"I agree." Layla grinned nervously. "Conor be the real wizard with those cabinets. Beautiful they are. I will owe him free shaving cream for a lifetime."

"Not that he would use it," Rhea muttered and had Layla laughing.

"Aye. I suppose not." She eyed the redheaded family friend, his scruffy beard a staple feature of his face. He swiped a sweaty hand over his brow and set his mouth in a firm line as he lifted a cabinet to the wall and began anchoring it. "He's a dear, that Conor."

"I agree. From what Riley tells me, the work here would not be moving as fast as it is without him."

"'Tis true. A work horse, our Conor. His mammy may have my head by the end of the week for not having him at the restaurant, but he does good work."

"The best," Rhea agreed.

Riley and Heidi walked up, their arms around one another. Rhea handed Riley a bottle of water and he chugged graciously. "Thanks for bringing this beauty by, Rhea darling." He handed the empty bottle back to her. "As much as I hate to release her, work calls me." He kissed Heidi once more and brushed her hair behind her ear. "I'll be seeing you later this evening, love."

"You bet you will." She squeezed him around the waist before he walked away. "That man..." She turned and leaned back against the counter as the other women watched with her. "I just love seeing him in a tool belt."

Chloe and Layla groaned as Rhea laughed.

"He's our brother, Heidi. Please don't." Layla held up her hand and turned as her name was called by Conor. She stepped over a pile of scrap wood and walked over to him. "What's the story, Conor?"

He heaved a tired sigh and motioned towards the remaining shelves and cabinets. "Just want to confirm placement of these, Layla. We have them in the design to stretch along this wall

here. I have a couple extra cabinets. You wish to have some the same height as the shelves or would you rather I anchor them next to the counter below?"

Layla rested her chin in her hands as she envisioned each choice. "Below."

"Below it is, then." He offered a tired smile and accepted the friendly pat to his shoulder as she made her way back towards the women. She paused briefly to watch two of Riley's men lift a heavy bookcase and carry it across the room. She wriggled her eyebrows at the women as the two muscled men set it down and moved about to their next task.

"Move along, sister," Murphy called from the ladder. "No good comes from ogling."

"Says the king of ogling," she challenged. "Mr. Shirtless on the ladder. No other man in here has their shirt off, Murphy. Why do you? Is it because you're nearest the window? Trying to drum up business for the pub later?"

He grinned. "It's a wee bit warm in here."

"Oh, I see." Layla bit back a grin as she swatted his pant leg on her way by him. "Well, being the good sister I am, I'd hate for you to faint from the heat." She opened the front door to the shop and anchored it with a brick as two good looking

females made their way up the footpath, their eyes drawn to Murphy in the window. As if they couldn't help themselves, their feet turned towards the flower shop. Layla chuckled to herself. "Like moths to a flame," she mumbled. Murphy greeted each woman happily, the blush to their cheeks confirming the reason they'd stepped inside. Chloe intercepted them and hustled them out of the way of the work crew and towards her half of the building. Rhea winked at Layla as if she knew the reason behind the women's visit.

"I've decided," Layla walked up to Rhea and continued watching the work before her. "For opening day, I'm going to have Murphy stand outside with a sign."

"Brilliant marketing plan," Rhea agreed. "You'd better make sure to have a full stock."

Layla laughed. "That is for certain. Speaking of which, I'm going to make me way to the B&B to work on just that."

"Taking over Sidna's kitchen? During the day? Rhea shook her head. "You're brave."

"'Tis bigger than the kitchen at me flat. She's agreeable. As long as I clean up my mess."

"Need help?"

"Would love some." Layla waved a hand to Chloe. "Heading to the B&B, sister," she called over the drills. Chloe waved from behind her counter and an accompanying Heidi did as well, and Rhea and Layla stepped outside into the fresh air.

∞

Delaney Hawkins slammed the receiver down on his desk phone and swiveled his chair around to face the row of cabinets behind him. He opened a file cabinet and filtered through the tabs of multiple manila folders until he landed on the one in which he sought. The Nifty Shop. "Ridiculous name," he grumbled, as he rolled his way back to his desk and plopped the file on top. Every year they complained about their taxes. Every year he had to review them and offer a second report whether the first accountant was wrong or not. And the accountant assigned to this client was Rhea Conners, so Delaney knew there would definitely be no mistakes. The best decision he'd made was hiring Rhea. Not only did she catch on quickly, she was thorough, honest, and efficient. Even now as he thumbed through the file, her neat handwriting and notes were easily readable and in perfect order. He slipped a paperclip off one of the stacks of documents and began to read. After only a minute, his cell phone rang. He looked down at the caller id and silenced the call. The last thing he wanted was for his best mate to interrupt his work. He knew he'd be talked into postponing the

file review and into a relaxing evening of golf. Which he needed, he reminded himself. But not today. Tax season wasn't over yet. Until then, he'd keep at it. He paused as he caught sight of a small notation Rhea had made. He squinted and couldn't make out the words. Without hesitation, he picked up his desk phone and dialed Rhea's personal phone number. She answered on the second ring.

"Rhea, sorry to bother you. Do you have a moment?" He heard the clanging of pots and pans and a woman's voice barking orders in the background. A muffled sound told him Rhea had dropped her phone. "So sorry, Delaney, yes. Yes, I have a minute. What can I do for you?"

"I had a brief question about a notation you've made in the Nifty Shop's file."

"Did they challenge the report again?" She sounded as exasperated as he felt.

"Yes."

"I'm sorry. I was hoping my detailed notes would help prevent that."

"With any regular person it would, Rhea. They are just difficult clients."

Another loud voice called in the background to Rhea. Covering the phone with her hand, he heard her muffled response. "Layla

O'Rifcan, if you do not stop yelling at me, so help me, I'll quit!" A sigh flooded the line. "So sorry Delaney. I'm helping a friend with some work and she's being quite bossy. Ouch." Rhea grimaced into the phone, Delaney envisioning the guilty party, a certain Layla, as the culprit for swatting her.

"No problem. I am sorry to call you during your time with friends and family. I was just confused about the small marks on page six," Delaney continued. He forced down his disappointment as another interruption caused Rhea to be distracted.

"I'm not sure which one you're talking about. Can you text me a picture of it? I might recognize it that way."

"Of course. I will do that." Relieved he might get an answer, he quickly set work to doing just that. "Did you receive it?"

"Just came through."

He waited patiently as Rhea studied the image.

"I can't tell. I can take a look at it Monday."

"I was really hoping to knock this out this evening," Delaney added.

Silence came over the line. He knew Rhea was particular about her time out of the office, especially since he knew her boyfriend lived in Castlebrook, a half hour away. She was more than

likely there with his family and her grandfather, but work was work. He needed her to explain the notation.

"Is it urgent?" she asked.

Lying, he grinned to himself, thankful that he was the boss and that she would come into the office if he said so. His hopes of a long weekend might be obtainable if he finished this file tonight. "Yes," he replied. "Urgent."

"Give me thirty minutes." She hung up on a sigh and a tinge of remorse had him stiffening his shoulders and continuing on with his study of the documents on his desk.

∞

"I don't understand, he let you leave early today, and now he's calling you back?" Layla shook her head. "Does the man not have any respect for family time?"

"It's fine. I'll dart back to the office, help him with the file, and be back before the family meal." Rhea grabbed her purse.

"Actually," Layla, knowing Rhea would end up staying at the office until late and then staying the night in Limerick instead of in Castlebrook, snatched her own purse. "I'm going with you."

"What?" Rhea looked stunned.

"He can't keep you longer than necessary if you have a friend waiting for you. And we can run by the little supply shop on the way home and I can grab more bottles."

Rhea's face split into a smile. "I like the way you think, Layla. Let's go. The sooner we get there, the sooner I can be rid of that Welshman's interruption to my weekend."

"Rightly said." Layla followed Rhea out of the B&B and towards Rhea's car. Climbing inside, she listened to the latest hits on the radio as Rhea drove, what was now, familiar roads to her.

It wasn't long before they pulled in front of a looming glass building. Rhea parked beside a small sports car in the front entry and hopped out. "You can wait in the car or come up."

"I'm coming. He has to see the friend in order to respect your time." Layla shoved the door open and stretched her legs.

"Alright, good point. It's this way." She opened the glass door and waited until Layla walked inside. Rhea flashed her badge towards a loan security guard as she headed towards the elevators.

"So important you are, Rhea, flashing your face card." Layla mumbled.

Rhea chuckled. "If only. That's just Henry so he doesn't require me to sign in every time." She pressed the button for the ninth floor.

Layla stood to the side resting against the hand rails of the elevator as she watched the numbers climb. When the doors opened, Rhea stepped out and turned left. A large lobby spread before them with lush leather sofas and colorful throw pillows. Plants graced every surface and vibrant canvases graced the walls. She may be aggravated with him for calling in Rhea during her time off, but Delaney had style when it came to the space, assuming he was the one who chose the décor.

Rhea walked down a narrow hall to a large office at the end that was all windows overlooking Limerick. She set her purse on the desk.

"This be your office, Rhea?"

"Yes."

Layla crossed her arms over her chest as she studied the space. Typical Rhea, the colors were neutral and scarcely decorated. There were, however, several photos of her and Clary gracing her desk and shelves.

"Give me just a second, and I'll show you around. I need to go see D—"

A knock sounded on the door frame and Rhea looked up. "Delaney," she finished.

Layla slowly turned and met the dark eyes of a lean face etched in a small scowl.

"Thanks for coming in Rhea." He handed her the file and she sat behind her desk, Delaney eased onto the top of it as he waited for her to flip through papers. "Delaney Hawkins," he extended a hand towards Layla.

"Oh right." Rhea held a hand to her forehead. "Delaney, this is Layla. Layla, this is Delaney."

"Layla O'Rifcan." Layla clasped his hand and firmly shook it making sure he knew of her disapproval at having Rhea come into the office.

"O'Rifcan? Are you a sister to Claron?"

"I am."

"Ah, I see. Well, lovely to meet you. I hear quite a bit about your family."

"I'm sure you do, as Rhea is one of us."

His lips quirked at her biting tone, but he remained cool. "I am sorry to interfere on family time."

"Are you?" Layla challenged.

Rhea cleared her throat in warning as she held up a paper. "Here's what the note was referring to. I counted this a loss for them considering the amount listed under repairs."

"Ah, I see." Delaney perused the paper, Layla staring at him. He was a handsome one, she'd add that to his favor. But a studious one. She might even classify him borderline geeky with his black framed glasses. But he was dressed in a fine suit, silk tie, and designer shoes. Despite his somewhat cold personality, he presented himself well. His brown hair was a bit long on top and had a bit of natural wave that she could tell had once been combed down, but due to a full work day at his desk with his hands running through it, it now sat in untamed waves with a touch of curl. He grunted in acknowledgment as Rhea continued explaining different aspects of the file they looked over and Layla eased into a chair and stared out over the city. Rhea had a nice setup here. She wondered if Clary knew how high up Rhea ranked amongst Mr. Delaney's employees. Did he realize she held a corner office with a view? It certainly explained why Rhea had yet to give up her position here. Why would she want to? She had a nice spot. Heidi, however, was up the hallway. Layla had noticed a small office with no window just up the hall from Rhea that had "Heidi Rustler" on the name plate. She was new, though, and Layla was glad the two friends were able to work together again. Heidi, after moving to Ireland from Texas, roomed with

Rhea and worked with her here in Limerick, and then both women made trips to Castlebrook over the weekend. Unless, of course, her brother Riley was working in Galway, and then Heidi made the trip there to see him.

It was funny, seeing her two older brothers so hopelessly in love. Odd though, too. She never envisioned such relationships for either of them. Not that she thought they wouldn't marry one day and have families, she just never exhausted herself over them matter. Now, here they were. Two incredible women turning them into mushy, lovesick puppies. She smiled to herself thinking of Clary and Rhea. Clary was always the tender-hearted one, and Rhea was perfect for him. Riley, well, he needed a fierce woman like Heidi to grab him by the hand and shake him up a bit. Both fit perfectly with her brothers and her family, and she was thankful she actually liked them both. Though she wasn't so sure about Heidi at first, she'd grown to love the bold Texan just as much as she loved sweet Rhea.

"Well, again," Delaney's Welsh-tinted accent interrupted Layla's line of thought. "I appreciate you coming in, Rhea. I'm sorry it was over something so trivial."

"No problem." Rhea stood and reached for her purse.

"While I have you here, I wonder if I might could pick your brain on a couple of other files." Delaney began walking towards the door expecting Rhea to follow. Layla caught the look of dread Rhea shot her way.

Layla stood and reached for her own purse. "Actually, Mr. Hawkins, Rhea and I will be on our way now."

Rhea's eyes slightly widened at Layla confronting her boss.

"It will only take a second, Rhea," he added, standing halfway in the office and in the hall.

"Perhaps another day. A work day." Layla shouldered past him. "Coming, Rhea? We have family to see to."

Rhea shrugged her shoulders towards Delaney. "She sort of takes the reins," she said softly.

"I can see that." Delaney offered a reassuring smile. "No worries though, Rhea. It is the start of your weekend. Enjoy your time and I will just have a list ready for you next week."

"Thanks, Delaney. You know, it would do you some good to take a break as well. Get out of this office. You're welcome to join us in Castlebrook." She walked with him towards the lobby where Layla

awaited patiently. Rhea saw Delaney's eyes quickly flicker over Layla.

"Perhaps another time, but thank you."

She patted his arm. "Have a good evening." Walking towards Layla, she draped her arm around the sister's waist and they made their way towards the elevator. "I'm proud of you for being so patient." He heard her mutter to the sister.

"I was almost at me breaking point."

"I could tell." Rhea chuckled as she pressed the button to await the elevator.

Delaney remained in the lobby, watching them. Layla shot him a quick glance and smiled. He frowned, a crease in his forehead appearing, as if he didn't know how to interpret such a friendly gesture. "Good day to you, Mr. Hawkins," she called as she stepped into the cart with Rhea and the doors closed on her satisfied smirk.

«CHAPTER TWO»

Rain. Nothing dampened his mood on a Friday evening more than rain. Why could Mother Nature not just refresh the earth when he was locked in an office all week? Why did she have to wait until he'd made plans to golf on Saturday? Or when he planned to drive around the countryside? Because she was a vixen. An unpredictable mass of emotions that sent the weather into a tailspin just for kicks. And here he sat, his car assaulted by fat drops of pummeling rain, debating on whether or not he should pull into the nearest village and wait out the storm or keep trudging through it. A pub sign highlighted against his windscreen and he quickly made the decision that a beer sounded much more appetizing than driving in the rain. He turned and

parked amongst other vehicles and cringed thinking of those who'd ventured out on the motorcycles that lined the front of the pub. They were in for a long wait. If he'd paid attention, he would know where he was, but he'd zoned out, too focused on the slippery road to know which village he'd journeyed into. He hopped out of the car and ran towards the door of the pub. He straightened his glasses and his shirt before opening the heavy wooden door and stepping inside.

The scent of wood polish, nuts, and ale filled his nostrils, and nothing could have been more appetizing. He slipped onto a stool at the bar.

"What's the criac there, friend?" A face appeared before him, a man with sandy colored hair and a smirk for a smile waited for Delaney to respond.

"Wet," he stated, his tone telling the barkeep he wasn't in the mood for banter.

"Ah, a pint for ye then?"

"Yes, please."

The man quickly made haste behind the kegs, the thick Guinness slowly pouring into a glass, the foamy head just rising to the top. A perfect pour. No spills. The barkeep slid it across the counter. "First time in Castlebrook?" he asked.

Delaney's brows rose. "Castlebrook?"

"Aye."

Delaney harrumphed under his breath as he took his first sip. "I didn't realize that's where I ended up."

The barkeep glanced down at his watch. "Traveling through?"

"You could say that. I live in Limerick. Was just taking a drive and got caught in the storm."

"Mother Nature, she can be a nasty beast that's for certain. Glad you ventured into me pub to wait out the storm. Feel free to yell if you need a top off." Murphy pointed to his half empty glass before venturing further down the bar.

The scent of perfumed woman dampened by rain filtered through the air and Delaney noticed several men at the bar straighten in their stools as a purse settled on top of the bar. A manicured hand pounded on the counter. "Hurry, Murphy, your sister has a throat on her."

Murphy swaggered towards the woman and tossed his towel over his shoulder and crossed his arms across his chest. "And will me sister be paying for her pint?"

"With a lovely smile and heartfelt thanks, like always."

Several of the men snickered. Delaney turned at the sound of a familiar voice. "And why are you in such a need for a pint, sister?"

"Rhea and Mam have booted me out of the kitchen in preparation of the meal. My work was confined to a corner of the island as it were, but Mammy had had enough. So, I'm at a standstill."

"Rhea did not wish to come see me? Pity." Murphy frowned.

"Clary walked in."

"Ah." Murphy laughed. "Lost for the rest of the evening, our Rhea."

"No doubt." Layla accepted the glass he slid across the counter and she sipped, her eyes wandering up and down the bar. She froze when she spotted Delaney. "Mr. Hawkins?"

Delaney straightened on his stool and met her silent survey. A slow smile spread across her face. Murphy looked from his sister to the stranger and waited for her to explain. She stood and walked to the stool next to him and sat, her hand resting on his shoulder. "Give this man another pint, Murphy, for he be a friend."

Murphy quickly busied himself making another draft so that he might obtain an introduction to the man his sister seemed intrigued to find sitting at

his bar. He brought it over and set it in front of the man.

"Brother, this be Delaney Hawkins."

Delaney, out of sheer society standards, extended his hand to Murphy, his hopes of quietly brooding into his beer now gone. The captivating woman beside him grinned. "This be our Rhea's boss in Limerick."

Murphy's eyes widened. "That so?"

"It's a pleasure," Delaney replied.

"And how do you like our sweet Rhea, Mr. Hawkins?" Murphy asked. "She be one of the best."

"That is true. Rhea is wonderful."

Murphy leaned his elbows on the bar as Layla draped an arm on Delaney's shoulder. The O'Rifcans were a bit intimidating in their friendly manner, Delaney thought. It made him shift uncomfortably. "Mr. Hawkins turned down an invitation to Castlebrook earlier today," Layla stated plainly. "Curious that you be sitting here now."

"Just trapped in the storm," Delaney clarified, taking a sip of his pint. Layla reached up and plucked his glasses off his face. Delaney straightened, appalled that she would do such a thing. She began polishing them with her shirt.

Murphy's grin widened as he watched the awkward man stare at his sister in bafflement. She looked at him. "Smudges from the rain." She studied his face a moment. "Not many a man can pull off glasses and then no glasses, but you can." She slipped them back on his face. "The exception also being our Clary." She patted his shoulder and then stood. "Thanks for the pint, Murphy. Should the rain continue, bring our Mr. Hawkins to the meal."

Murphy saluted in obedience.

"Have a care, Mr. Hawkins." Layla slid her purse onto her shoulder and made her way to the door. Every man's head turned as she exited, and Delaney's gaze ventured back towards the brother whose smirk grew to a full-fledged grin. "So, what say you, Mr. Hawkins? Fancy a bite?"

∞

The Bed and Breakfast, bearing the name of Sidna, looked to be a charming place. He found it quaint, colorful, and fragrant as he hurried up the walkway behind Murphy. He was a fool for coming. And what was meant to be a welcoming red door for guests, Delaney took as the signal to stop. What was he thinking? Rhea would no doubt be disappointed with him for infringing upon her time away from the office. Though she had extended an invitation to Castlebrook, he doubted she meant with her family. So why was he here?

He didn't have time to think his decision through, however, as Murphy opened the door and welcomed him inside.

"Hello to the family!" Murphy called. Several heads looked up from a game of cards in the sitting room. All eyes on Delaney.

"And who do we have here?" An older woman, plump and primed with dish towel and flour-covered hands stood to the side of the room by another doorway, hands on her hips.

"This be—"

"Delaney?" Rhea's surprised voice carried through the room as she poked her head through the door behind the older woman. The lady moved and allowed Rhea access to the room. Rhea walked forward, her shock evident as she greeted him with a friendly hug. "What made you decide to come to Castlebrook?"

"Ah, well, that was unplanned, I'm afraid."

Murphy slapped him on the back as if they were old friends. "Wandering the back roads and got caught in the rain. Much like you, Rhea. Good thing he wandered into the best establishment in the village."

"I see." Rhea waved him forward. "Well, come in. Let me introduce you to everyone." She pointed to

a beautiful redhead sitting on the sofa holding a pair of kings as her opponent shuffled their own cards in their hand. "That's Chloe." The woman waved and smiled. Delaney gave a brief nod.

"That's Riley. You've heard of him via Heidi at work."

"Of course. The architect." Delaney stepped forward and shook Riley's hand.

"Nice to meet you, Mr. Delaney. Many thanks to you for employing our Rhea and my Heidi." Riley took his seat once more as Rhea turned him towards an elderly gentleman sitting in a plump chair, a cane resting against the side. "This is my grandpa, Roland."

"Pleasure." Delaney shook the man's hand.

"Clary!" A booming voice called from the kitchen doorway. "Best hurry in here. Rhea's got a lad on her arm that's not you! And he's already meeting the family!" Rhea turned to see Jaron grinning as he stepped out of a curious Claron's path. Claron's furrowed brow cleared into a welcoming smile. Delaney, a bit relieved at the sight of another familiar face, extended his hand.

"Delaney, welcome to Castlebrook. Didn't realize you were coming for the meal."

"A bit of a last-minute decision," Delaney replied.

"Glad you've come." Claron slapped him on the back as he walked towards an empty spot on the couch next to Chloe. Rhea continued introducing him to every face— so many faces— that walked into the room. But one was missing. Layla. He hated that he noticed that. And he also didn't quite like that he felt disappointed by her absence.

"Whereabouts are you from, Mr. Delaney?" Claron Senior, a tall, boisterous man with a friendly disposition, called from his chair opposite the room. "Can't quite place that accent, I'm afraid."

"Wales," Delaney replied. "Though I grew up in Limerick."

"That would explain the blend then." Mr. O'Rifcan smiled. "I like him. Give him a seat, Murphy."

Murphy pulled up an empty wooden chair and placed it near Rhea's grandfather. "What's your drink, Mr. Delaney?"

Delaney looked at the other glasses in the room and noted most were a red wine. "Wine is fine, thank you. And it's just Delaney."

Murphy disappeared, and Rhea walked back into the room and squeezed herself between Chloe and Claron on the couch. Claron kissed her sweetly on the lips when she sat.

"I'm glad to see you got out of the office for the weekend, Delaney," Rhea said.

"Once I finished the second look at the file we discussed, I realized everything else could wait until Monday."

"Good." Rhea took a sip of her own glass as Murphy appeared and handed Delaney his.

"Who touched my bottles?" An angry voice called from the kitchen as the door swung open and a fuming Layla hurried into the sitting room. "Fess up. I need to know who the guilty party is so as to direct my vengeance. All my mixtures spilt and are now a waste thanks be to the culprit. Now who did it?" She fisted her hands on her hips as her eyes surveyed each person in the room. They landed on the back of Delaney's head. He felt the daggers before he even turned. When his eyes met hers, surprise mixed with her current fury.

"Was not me, I just arrived." Murphy held up his hands. "And I know better than to mess with your glass."

"As you should," She barked. "Jaron?"

"Not me. I stay far away from the kitchen unless it is for sampling."

Her temper only flaring more, Layla stomped her foot and a loud pop sounded in the

air. Squealing from the slap of the towel on her backside, Layla turned to find her mother firmly planted behind her. "Stop yer bullying, Layla. 'Twas me who moved your bottles and mixes. Sorry they took a tip, but you do not go around me house yellin' at everybody for your own fault of not moving them when asked. Now get in the kitchen and help with preparations." Layla, baffled her mother had swatted her, turned and stomped her way into the kitchen. Mrs. O'Rifcan smiled down at Delaney. "Now, Mr. Delaney," she said sweetly, making several chuckles filter about the room at her sudden mood shift towards a guest. "Are you a fan of lamb?"

∞

She was rarely embarrassed. Rarely awkward around people, especially men, but with Delaney Hawkins, Layla found herself completely fidgety. He stared. She caught him several times studying her as if she held the secrets to the world. Not that she minded men staring. In fact, she usually wished for them to do so, but not Delaney. He wasn't her type. Too serious. Too wiry of build. And arrogant. The way he sat now as if he ruled from on high: shoulders back, that pointed chin slightly lifted. His glasses hid his expression, but the scowl on his face made her think he wished to be anywhere than at the O'Rifcan table.

"So, Mr. Delaney," Chloe began, "How is it working with Rhea and Heidi? Have they made you gone mad yet?" She giggled as Heidi nudged her.

Delaney forced a polite smile. "Not at all. They are hard workers, which is much appreciated."

"Boring," Jaron chimed in. "Crunching numbers all day."

"Boring?" Heidi playfully challenged. "And who was it bringing me his receipts in a shoebox not but a month ago, begging me to 'crunch his numbers'?"

Jaron flushed and then chuckled. "'Tis true enough."

"We each have our gifts," Sidna chimed in. "Best be grateful for those whose differ from our own."

"Speaking of gifts," Riley added. "This lamb is superb, Mammy."

Mrs. O'Rifcan straightened in pride.

"That it is," Claron agreed, along with other mumbles of agreement along the table.

"I have Rhea to thank for that. She found this lovely spice combination in Limerick and brought it for me to try."

Claron lightly squeezed Rhea's knee and winked at her for thinking of his mother. Delaney watched their interaction with guarded interest.

"Do you cook much, Mr. Delaney?" Chloe asked.

"Why so many questions, sister?" Layla interrupted.

Chloe, never breaking stride, met Layla's glare head on. "He's a guest. I'm attempting to make him feel welcome. Unlike the surly bat at the end of the table." Layla's jaw dropped at the insult, but the brothers all began to laugh.

As Chloe turned back to listen to Delaney's response, a pea flew from Layla's hand and pelted Chloe in the cheek. Her hand flew up in surprise to block the next assault. "Layla Aideen!" she gasped in embarrassment.

Mr. O'Rifcan slammed a hand on the table and had everyone jumping in their seats. "Enough!" he bellowed. Turning his gaze towards Delaney, he waved for the man to answer.

Delaney cleared his throat. "The answer would be a no, I'm afraid. I do not cook much."

"Such a shame." Sidna tisked her tongue. "Just know you are always welcome to a seat at our table should you find yourself in need of a meal."

"That is very kind, Mrs. O'Rifcan. Thank you."

"It's Sidna, love. And it's a pleasure. Typically, our table does not house such hostility. But I'm afraid I soured Layla's mood."

"*My* mood?" Layla set her fork down. "I believe I'm finished and will head home. I have no desire to sit here and be bullied by the lot of ye." She grabbed a bread roll as she stood. "Rhea, find me tomorrow. You can help me with my mixes." She turned a fiery gaze towards Delaney. "It was a pleasure, Mr. Delaney."

Everyone watched as she exited through the kitchen and out the back door.

A low whistle sounded from down the table and Declan bit back a smirk. "You've got a temper going there, Mammy," he teased.

"She'll be fine. She knows not to leave a mess in me kitchen. 'Tis the stress of her new business that sits upon her shoulders right now. Once she grows accustomed to it, she'll be back to her usual ways."

"New business?" Delaney asked.

"Layla is opening a shop that sells lotions, soaps, candles, and such," Rhea explained. "She makes them all herself."

"Gifted to be certain," Jace said, sliding a hand over his smooth jaw.

"Aye. Agreed. Denise likes the smooth chin," Tommy piped up, his grin spreading at the mention of his new girlfriend's name.

"Denise O'Malley," Murphy stated. "I will admit she is one lass that slipped through me fingers. Who'd have thought she would have turned out to be such a beauty."

"Easy brother," Tommy warned.

Murphy held up his hands and grinned in surrender.

"Aye," Riley agreed. "Remember that dreadful hair cut she once had?" He grimaced and laughed at the blow to the chest from Heidi's hand swatting him.

"I think we have all had bad hair days in the past," Rhea added. "I know I did. Thankfully, my mom decided she was not the best hairdresser. Eventually."

Claron lightly tugged on her silky hair. "Would be a crime to mess this up," he whispered. Rhea flushed as she caught Delaney watching them.

She cleared her throat. "So how long do you plan on staying in Castlebrook, Delaney?"

Annoyed that the attention had somehow fluttered back to him, he rested his fork on the edge of his plate, to signal he was finished with his

meal. "Not long. I imagine I will head home once the rain lets up."

"Not likely," Riley stated. "Supposed to be a slosher, I'm afraid."

"Oh heavens." Sidna looked to Riley.

"Don't worry, Mam. I'm not driving back to Galway or Limerick tonight. I'm crashing at Clary's."

"Is that so?" Claron asked.

Riley nodded. "Of course. Can't a brother invite himself over?"

"I suppose I'll allow it."

"Good." Riley looked to Delaney. "How about it, Delaney?"

"I'm sorry?" Delaney asked.

"How about waiting out the storm at Clary's? He's plenty of room. Or here at the B&B, right, Mam?"

"Oh, of course. Plenty of rooms upstairs. Rhea be in suite 2, Heidi in suite 3. But I have number four open if you need, Mr. Delaney."

"Much appreciated, but I will just head home."

"Not in this weather, lad," Mr. O'Rifcan said. "The roads will be too slick and muddy for traveling.

Best stay with the boys so as not to be driven mad by the females."

"Driven mad?" Sidna chortled. "As if you don't love having us all cluck about you."

He winked at Heidi and Rhea and had them grinning. "Clary and Riley will take good care of ye for the night. Right, lads?"

The brothers nodded.

Rhea could tell Delaney felt cornered. The fear he tried to hide almost made her laugh if she didn't feel so sorry for him. "Will be good for you, Delaney," she whispered across the table. "A break from the city."

"I suppose you're right. I guess I could be up for a little adventure in the country."

"Settled then." Mr. O'Rifcan banged his fist on the table like a gavel. "Now, Sidna, my love, what's for dessert?"

«CHAPTER THREE»

The small cottage welcomed him with open windows and billowing drapes as Claron hurried about the room shutting windows. "I'd forgotten I'd raised the windows earlier," he grumbled as Riley helped lower a couple of windows as well. "Fetch a towel, will you, brother?" Claron called over his shoulder as he stretched over the couch to close the windows behind it. A scratching noise came from the back door and Claron opened it to a pitiful Rugby, his Irish Setter. One tail swish and whine later, Rugby was inside, along with Holstein, the barn cat. Rugby rushed towards Delaney, excited over the prospect of someone new. "Easy, Rugby," Claron warned. "You've the need to make a positive impression. This be Rhea's boss." Rugby, as if

understanding his owner's request, sat perfectly by Delaney's feet and raised his right paw to shake.

"Bloody genius," Delaney muttered, as he shook the friendly dog's extended paw.

"He has his moments." Claron turned from the windows and caught the towel Riley tossed his way as both brothers ran the dry cloths over wet floors. "I've been meaning to mop. Rhea will be grateful." He grinned as Riley laughed.

"She will not be pleased with just rain water for washing, Clary."

"It be our secret then, brother." Claron walked towards his kitchen, tossing the wet towel towards his washing machine. "What will it be? Beer? Wine? Whiskey?" Claron looked towards Delaney.

"Honestly, I could use a good toss back of whiskey."

"Whiskey 'tis then."

"Good choice." Riley tossed his towel in the same direction as Claron's. "After Layla's sour mood, I could use a bit of a pick me up."

"What was that about?" Perplexed about his sister, Claron shook his head. "Mam be right about the stress of trying to start her business, but tonight was a bit much."

"Oh, I'm sure she had a lad cancel dinner plans on her or something." Riley took a sip from his glass and let the first burn of the alcohol slide down his throat. He sighed. "That be a good one."

Delaney did the same and found the extra warmth from the whiskey was welcome against his chilled hands. "Damp clothes, warm whiskey. Doesn't get much better than that."

Claron nodded in agreement as Holstein jumped into a chair and meowed. "Ah, of course." He petted the cat's head and walked towards a metal pail with lid and opened it to scoop a large cup full of food for the cat. He poured it into a small bowl.

"I appreciate you giving me somewhere to stay for the night, Claron."

"Of course. 'Tis not a problem a'tall. If I'm being honest, I think Rhea is pleased. She's mentioned to me several times how she would like you to visit Castlebrook."

"Really?"

"Aye. Glad we could make it happen despite the rain."

"Bit of a workaholic, Del?" Riley asked.

"It's Delaney," he corrected. "And yes. I enjoy my work."

Riley bit back a smirk as he cast a glance towards his brother at the man's snooty attitude. "I love me work as well, but 'tis nice to spend my weekends with Heidi. Nothing better than a beautiful woman to spend some free time with. Right, brother?"

"Agreed. Though Rhea is more patient with me than I deserve."

"That she is." Riley pulled out a chair at the kitchen table and sat, Delaney and Claron following suit.

"Sweet Rhea embracing the farm life." Riley shook his head. "Poor thing."

"She loves it almost as much as I do," Claron replied.

"For now, brother. But if you wait too much longer to bejewel that lass she might lose interest."

"I doubt that," Delaney said behind his glass before he took a sip. "She talks of it constantly. You, the dairy, the farming, the family."

A tender smile washed over Claron's face. "That's good to hear."

"I must admit I dread the day she quits to be in Castlebrook fulltime. I know it's coming, but I just can't envision the office without her. She's my best accountant."

"Why would she quit?" Claron asked.

"Oh brother, you eejit." Riley laughed. "Because she will end up marrying you and living on the farm. And we all know once that happens, the two of you will be hopeless apart from one another."

Claron shook his head. "I do not wish for her to give up her work. She enjoys it."

"It's her decision, though, isn't it?" Delaney asked.

"Well, of course." Claron straightened his shoulders as if Delaney were challenging him. "Rhea is free to make her own decisions. I would just hate for her to give up a job she loves to live on the farm and what? Help me?"

"I'm sure she would find a way to be useful," Riley added.

"For certain, she is a help when she is here, but I do not wish for it to become an obligation for her."

Delaney listened as the two brothers discussed Rhea. It felt odd, discussing her personal life without her present. Though, he did have to admit, he enjoyed seeing a part of her life she did talk about so much. He wasn't a family man. He wasn't particularly close with his parents, and he had no siblings. So the thought of someone wishing to surround themselves with family all the time baffled him.

"And what of my Heidi, Delaney? How is she to work with?" Riley asked curiously.

"She's good as well, but still learning the ropes. She also has a bit of a mouth on her at times."

Riley grinned proudly. "That she does. A wildfire, my Heidi."

"I'm grateful to Rhea for bringing her on board." Delaney continued. "With time, I feel she will be a great fit."

"Must be nice, working with beautiful women every day," Riley continued, curious as to what made Delaney Hawkins relax. Talk of women? Whiskey? Perhaps sports? He cringed, realizing his sport's knowledge was a bit rusty. Clary would need to carry that conversation should it arise.

"I suppose it's fine," Delaney replied.

"Fine?" Both O'Rifcan brothers asked in surprise.

Claron shook his head. "Beats a bunch of cows."

"Or sweaty men," Riley countered.

"Aye, beat me there, brother." Claron laughed.

"Out of the three of us, I believe Mr. Delaney wins when it comes to coworkers." Riley tipped his head towards Delaney.

Delaney sipped his whiskey in silence. The brothers were amiable enough, he thought. But he just wasn't in a talkative mood. He set his empty glass down on the table. Claron reached for the bottle of whiskey but Delaney waved his hand. "No thank you, Claron. One was more than enough."

"It's Friday, lad. Have another." Riley grabbed the bottle and poured Delaney another glass and tapped his against it. Reluctantly, Delaney took the newly filled glass.

"Wonder how Murphy is faring at the pub." Riley swirled the amber liquid in his glass and took another sip. "Probably crowded due to the weather. Everyone needing a wee pick me up."

"More than likely," Claron agreed. "But noisy."

"So noisy," Riley concurred. "One thing I don't miss about the pub on a Friday. Were the women going?"

Shrugging, Claron sipped. "Rhea didn't mention it."

"Ah, perhaps they are trying to work wonders on Layla. Or maybe they're helping make her brews and potions."

"I doubt she lets them create anything." Claron quirked a grin. "Rhea says Layla is rather a perfectionist. All Rhea has been able to do is fill bottles, and even then, Layla comes along behind

her to pour a little out or add a little more, she says."

"I'm surprised at that. Never saw our Layla as a perfectionist. Perhaps she's maturing. Now that it is her own work, she is willing to work a bit harder."

"Owning one's business is always a challenge," Delaney added. "Hopefully family support will encourage her."

"Oh, she has the family's support," Riley explained. "If it weren't for Chloe's patience," he placed a hand on his chest. "Bless her."

"The redheaded sister?" Delaney asked.

"Aye. That be the one."

"What has she done?"

"She be the town florist, you see," Riley elucidated. "And she's allowing me to come in and tear up half her shop so as to remodel it for Layla to have a business space."

Amazement settled on Delaney's features. "That is kind, indeed."

"Aye. But that's our Chloe. Always wishing to help someone out. No kinder heart in Castlebrook."

"Except maybe Conor," Claron added.

"Ah, yes. Good 'ol Conor. Can't forget'im."

"And who is this Conor? I've heard Rhea mention the name," Delaney asked.

"Friend of the family." Claron took a sip of his whiskey and finished off his glass. "Always willing to serve, Conor is."

"A jolly one too," Riley mentioned. "Best get to know all of us, Mr. Delaney. It would seem our Rhea wishes to make you social with us."

"I have no idea why. Most employees wish to keep their work life separate from their personal life."

"Not Rhea," the brothers said in unison.

"I'm starting to see that. I hate to disappoint her, but if it weren't for the weather, I would not be in Castlebrook at all. I tend to be one of those that likes to keep his work and personal life separate."

"And what do you like to do in your personal time?" Riley asked. "Do you have a lass?"

"No." Delaney nudged his half empty glass to the side and clasped his hands atop the table as if it were his desk. "I golf, mostly."

Riley's brows rose in acknowledgement, but he did not say anything waiting for Delaney to continue. When he didn't, he cast a glance at his brother. Clary did not disappoint.

"Is that it?" Curious, Claron eyed Delaney warily.

"Mostly. I do not have that much time away from the office. Being the business owner and all."

"Well, I say lad, it's a good thing the weather betrayed you tonight. Perhaps we can convince you to join us again at the pub for a plain sometime. Get you out of Limerick." Claron nudged Rugby under the table and the dog lazily rolled to his side and rested his head on Claron's foot.

Delaney said nothing. He was tired of conversation. Yes, he golfed. Yes, it was enough. Why did the brothers seem to think he needed more to do in his spare time? He enjoyed his way of things. Work. Home. Golf. He didn't really need much else. He was a simple man. Yet, when the brother's conversation steered towards their women again, Delaney felt awkwardly lacking. The feeling turned sour in his belly and he stood. "I think I will call it a night, if that's alright?"

"Of course." Claron stood. "Let me show you the way to your room."

Riley toasted the two men as they stood, while he continued to sit at the table and sip on his drink. A few minutes later, Claron walked back into the kitchen.

"He's an odd one," Riley murmured.

"More like a stiff one."

Riley chuckled at his brother's honest assessment. "Aye. Not sure he knows how to relax. Interesting that your Rhea has taken a liking to him."

"Rhea tends to want to help those who need it."

"True. A sweetheart, your Rhea."

"Aye. She is."

"He's a hard man though, Clary. Perhaps we should try to convince her not to set her hopes too high."

Grunting in agreement, Claron walked his empty glass to the sink. "Knowing Rhea, however, she will just try harder."

"And what a fun challenge he will be for her." Riley grinned. "Should be fun to see what becomes of Mr. Delaney."

∞

"Just grind the petals down, Rhea." Layla dropped more of the lavender petals into the mortar as Rhea gently used the pestle to bring out their fragrance. "That's it. Slow and easy. Can't rush magic." She grinned as she turned to grab a jar off the top shelf. Her new shelves. Yes, the flower shop was still a total disaster, but her cabinets and work space were set and ready for use. All that was left were the display shelves.

Conor worked diligently as the women continued their work on bath salts.

Rhea paused in her smashing. "It's going to look incredible in here, Layla. I already love being in here. Chloe's flowers, your candles and lotions. Despite the sweaty men that have been wandering in and out, it smells fresh and feminine. It's bright and cheery." She motioned to the windows where the dreary rain from the day before had parted just enough for an early morning sun. "I think you O'Rifcan sisters are going to knock'em dead."

"I thought I did that already." Layla jested as she opened the lids to several small jars.

Rhea laughed. "True. But in a totally different way."

Layla's smile slightly faltered before she set the last jar on the counter and turned towards Rhea. "Do you think I'm crazy for wanting to do all this?" She waved her hand around the destructed shop.

"Not at all." Rhea gently squeezed Layla's arm. "I'm proud of you for doing this. You have a gift, Layla, and I think it is wonderful that you want to share it with others."

"I hadn't thought of it like that. I must admit, my motives have been slightly more selfish than that. I honestly am just ready to do something other than

waitressing for Mam." She bent down to open one of the lower cabinets to fetch a wooden cutting block and set it on the counter.

"I don't think wanting more for yourself is necessarily selfish. It can be, but I don't believe it is in this case," Rhea added. "Don't be so hard on yourself."

"I've just felt stuck," Layla confessed. "I love Castlebrook, don't get me wrong, but I've felt stifled. All me other siblings have their successes, their careers, loves, families, and I have what? A place at the table? I want more than that. And I know for certain I do not wish to wait around any longer for it to just fall in me lap."

Rhea quietly continued grinding petals as she listened.

"I look at you and Heidi, even Chloe... you three have your lives perfectly laid out." Layla held up her hand to ward off Rhea's interruption. "No, no. I know you have all had your own hurdles to get to this point, but my point is that you three found what you wanted in life and went after it. You wished for a fresh start here in Ireland and you did it. Heidi wished to grab Riley by his luscious locks and make him hers, and she did it. Chloe, me own younger sister, has always wanted to work with her flowers, and look at the success she's made of herself." Layla pointed to Chloe's half of the shop, the tidy space reflecting the delicate care Chloe

showcased to all areas of her life. "I'm just a mess compared to all of you."

"Not true. You have incredible talents and gifts," Rhea defended. "Look at what you're doing right now." She pointed to the flowers in her bowl and to Layla absentmindedly mixing her own concoction of herbs. "You manage Claron's house when you rent it out. That was your idea and look how successful it is when he actually lets you do it. You work for Sidna and the customers love you. I think you are definitely selling yourself short. You're brazen, bold, and beautiful. The world is your oyster." Rhea giggled at the last phrase. "Sorry, that saying always makes me laugh, though it was all I could think of. The point is, Layla, that you can do whatever you set your mind to. And I'm excited for you because I'm finally seeing you set your mind to something you're passionate about. You're going to rock this business."

Layla eased onto a stool as she continued to splice through the stems of fresh Rosemary. Quiet, she reflected on Rhea's words. She set her knife down and reached over to squeeze Rhea's hand. "Thank you, Rhea."

"You don't have to thank me for pointing out the obvious." Rhea set her pestle down. "Now are you going to tell me what to do with this stuff, because I feel like I've ground this to oblivion."

Layla laughed and nodded. "Aye, that's how you know you're done. Here, let me take it." As she reached for the mortar, the bell above the door rang and Chloe waltzed inside carrying a paper grocery bag and set it upon her counter. "Morning all."

"Morning," the two women replied and heard Conor echo the sentiment. Both women had forgotten his presence and Layla immediately flushed, realizing he'd more than likely overheard their previous conversation. Though he didn't say anything, his eyes met hers as he lifted another shelf into place.

"I brought you a strong brew, Conor, in thanks for your early start." Chloe walked over and handed him a paper cup with lid. "Your mammy said it was your favorite. I hope she is right, for I am hoping it butters you up for a large request."

"And what request might that be?" Conor took a sip and his brows rose at the stout liquid. It was a bit stronger than his liking, but the hopeful glint in Chloe's eyes had him holding his tongue on his tastes.

"It doesn't have to be right away," she began. "But when you're done with Layla's shelves, I wondered if I could have you look at a design for me?"

"I could have a look." Conor set his drill down.

"Oh, not now. Please." Chloe looked cautiously at Layla. "I wish for you to finish your work for Layla first. Afterwards, if you're up for another O'Rifcan project, I would like to show you."

"Aye, that be the way of it then. I should be wrapping up Layla's shelves today. The building, at least. You wish to color the wood, Layla?"

"Aye. A nice rich color, to match Chloe's till counter."

He nodded in understanding. "I can do that. You O'Rifcans will have me mammy looking for new help at the restaurant here soon." He laughed heartily as he lifted another long shelf with ease and set it upon the brackets he'd drilled into the walls.

"A long chat I had with her just now," Chloe stated as she walked back towards her grocery bag and withdrew a case of minerals. She offered one to the other women and they nodded. Rhea eagerly popped the tab on the soda and drank. The sisters watched her in amusement.

"What?" she asked on a satisfied sigh. "I was thirsty."

"And what did Conor's mammy have to say?" Layla asked, urging Chloe to continue.

"Oh, right." Chloe took a sip of her own drink and sat on a vacant stool. "Just that she was grateful we'd chosen Conor as our carpenter."

"Well, who else would we choose?" Layla asked in bafflement. "He be the best in the county."

Conor's cheeks flushed as he turned back to his work. Rhea smiled tenderly at his back. The robust man also had the kindest and softest heart in the county too.

"Between us and Clary, you might have a full season of work ahead of you," Chloe continued.

"Claron?" Rhea asked. "What project does he have you working on, Conor?"

Chloe's face blanched and Layla shot her a nervous glance as Conor fumbled over how to respond.

"Oh, I'm sure Clary has fence posts or something that need tendin'." Layla waved her hand nonchalantly. "Boring farm work, I'm sure." She nodded for Conor to agree and the man just rummaged through his tool chest.

"Oh. That's probably true. He did mention something like that the other day," Rhea added, oblivious to the tension amongst the others about revealing a potential secret. Conor found Chloe and Layla staring at him and he bit back a smile as he continued working. "And his farm work is not

boring," Rhea added, always quick to defend Claron.

Layla laughed and Chloe grinned. "Oh Rhea love, only a woman in love would say such a thing."

"Well, I am in love with him, so yes." Rhea fisted her hand on her hip. "Speaking of his work, I believe Riley was to help him milk this morning. Delaney was still sleeping last I talked with him. I'm curious to see if they can convince Delaney to hang around Castlebrook the rest of the weekend or if he will hurry his way back to Limerick and burrow himself back into his shell."

"An odd man, your Mr. Delaney," Chloe admitted. "All tense and brooding."

"He doesn't quite know how to be social," Rhea explained.

"Oh, that was quite obvious last night." Chloe shrugged. "Quite sad really. He'd be a handsome sort if he were to choose a smile every now and then."

"Did he smile a'tall last night?" Layla asked. "I left too early to witness it if he did."

"That would be a no." Chloe began unpacking her grocery bag and set out a loaf of bread and other ingredients for sandwich making to stock the

small kitchen in the back of her shop for days she did not go home to eat.

"He's just a bit tense around new people." Rhea handed Layla the pestle as Layla pointed to the tools on the other side of the counter from her.

"Perhaps a night with the boys loosened him up," Chloe encouraged.

"Or it was poor torture," Layla added. "Clary *and* Riley? I imagine all they did was talk about their females and bore Mr. Delaney to tears."

"And what is wrong with their females?" Rhea's leading tone had the sisters laughing.

"Nothing a'tall, dear Rhea. Just that our brothers have not been able to talk of anything else since you and Heidi have stolen their hearts. And to a man like Mr. Delaney, I imagine that sort of talk is not quite his interest."

"He is a bit awkward when the talk of relationships comes into play," Rhea admitted. "Even at work, if I mention plans I have with Claron, Delaney fidgets and quickly nudges me out the door or changes the subject. I don't think he has many close relationships in his life."

"All business, that one," Chloe agreed. "I don't even have to know him, and I see that."

"All business is not a bad thing," Layla pointed out. "That's how I wish to be the next few months."

"You? All business?" Chloe asked, her brows rising, and her bright green eyes sparkled in amusement. "And after a long day at the store, where is it you plan to go?"

"Murphy's Pub, of course," Layla stated.

"A social place," Chloe quipped. "I doubt Mr. Delaney unwinds at a bar after a long day's work."

"No. At least not that I know of. I've seen him receive calls from friends, but he's always turned them down." Rhea nodded. "He either stays late at the office longer than anyone else or heads to his house. He never goes out with any of us for happy hour. Sticks to himself."

"That is all business," Chloe pointed out. "No mingling with his co-workers, no socializing outside the office. That will not be you, sister. You're too much of a social butterfly for such a life."

Layla frowned as she thought about it. "I do love me a pint after a long day. I don't think I could give that up."

"And you shouldn't have to," Rhea confirmed. "It's healthy to have a life outside of work. It's my hope

that this weekend will convince Delaney to do it more often."

"That is, if Clary and Riley don't scare him off." Chloe chuckled at her own comment and had the other two women laughing in response.

"Aye, he survived Murphy at the pub. If he survived the night at Clary's, then I'd say Mr. Delaney is made of firmer stuff than we give him credit for." Layla grinned.

"We shall see. Oh Lord, please don't let him be scarred for life." Rhea framed her face with her hands in new worry as Chloe and Layla burst into laughter.

«CHAPTER FOUR»

Delaney stood back and watched as the two brothers rotated the group of cows before him. He was appalled. The stench, the grime, and the work itself held him frozen in the corner of the milk barn. Riley tossed an excrement covered towel towards him. He sidestepped to avoid it slapping against his white button up shirt from his previous day at work. He did not have a spare change of clothes, so here he stood in his suit and tie, prepared more for a day at the office than a morning spent milking cows. The only difference was the set of clunky rubber boots Claron had given him to wear. The brother had offered him a set of clothes fit for the barn, but Delaney would not settle for clothes that were not his own. Now he regretted his decision as the towel landed by

his feet. "Sorry there, Del." Riley flashed an innocent grin. "Was aiming for the bucket." He pointed to the bucket full of sludge that sat next to his feet. Delaney ground his teeth as he tucked his fists into his pockets. The brother insisted on calling him Del, which he despised, and he knew full well the aim was not an accident.

Claron worked silently and swiftly, only scowling when Riley caused an interruption in his routine. Delaney respected Rhea's man. No one could deny the work was tedious—and disgusting—but Claron worked diligently, his calm temperament transferring to the cows before him. The work fit the man perfectly. Rhea had said as much, but to see him in action was another thing all together. Delaney respected hard workers. Especially when they seemed to love the work they did, and Claron did both. Riley, however, he wasn't so sure about. He knew the brother was an architect. He'd heard of his work, seen some of it as well, but he wasn't quite sure of the man just yet. Before the ungodly hour to start milking—that they had somehow convinced him to tag along for— Riley had showcased his current drafts of Claron's cottage. The detailed sketches outlining the changes the youngest brother wished to make to accommodate Rhea in his future were splendid. The small cottage was already a stunning space on top of Angel's Gap, but with the suggested changes Riley had drafted, the house would be a beacon of pure Irish beauty. The all-glass backside

overlooking the cliffs and the River Shannon would bring the beautiful outdoors in, and Delaney could not fathom having the striking view as an everyday scene to wake up to. Rhea would most definitely never wish to leave. And that thought depressed him more than the brown smudge that had somehow found its way onto his white shirt.

"Hey Del, can you hand me that hose there?" Riley asked, pointing to a long red hose behind Delaney. Delaney unwrapped the hose and walked it towards Riley. He hesitantly handed it over in fear the brother may turn it on him. Instead, Claron pointed at a bucket by his feet and Riley filled it up. He then handed the hose back to Delaney to take back to its original position. Claron dipped a set of teat cups in the refreshed bucket and then slipped them onto the cow before him. Delaney wrapped the hose back against the wall as Holstein, Claron's cat, wound around his ankles. He lightly nudged the cat with his boot. He hated cats. The purring creature looked up at him adoringly as he continued to wind himself through Delaney's slacks. He heard a shuffle of hooves and glanced up to see the last rotation of cows circle out of the barn. They were finished. Relief washed over him as he ached to breathe fresh air again. Riley motioned towards him. "We can get started on the next task while Clary wraps it up in here. Come along."

Dread pitted in Delaney's stomach as he followed Riley towards a manure covered lot behind the barn. "We need to feed the calves." Riley motioned to a small room where large steel containers sat, and milk flooded into them through a set of pipes. Riley disconnected a pipe and fresh milk spilled into two large buckets. He refastened the hose and reached for an oversized bottle. "This be our Rhea's favorite part, feeding the babes," Riley explained. Delaney watched him assemble the first bottle.

"You plan on helping?" Riley asked.

Delaney hopped to attention. "Yes, of course." He cleared his throat. "Just watching to see how you preferred it done."

Riley stifled a smile as he watched the anxious man fill a bottle. When they'd filled and fastened all the bottles before the calves, Riley rested his hands on his hips. "Imagine doing this twice a day every day."

"I can't," Delaney admitted. "Nor would I want to."

"Aye. I agree. Clary be good for it, though. Loves farming, he does. Been in his blood since we were lads. I typically avoid helping, but considering he gave me a roof over my head last night, I felt I owed it to him."

"True. Now that the storms have passed, I can head back to Limerick. And shower." Delaney took a whiff of his shirt and shuddered.

Riley laughed and slapped him heartily on the back. "We'll take you to fetch your wheels. I imagine Murphy has kept a close eye on it at the pub." Riley led the way back to the cottage, Claron just ahead of them waiting at his vehicle. The white truck beckoned Delaney's feet in hopes that he would soon be headed home to peace and quiet. Without invitation, he opened the door to the backseat and climbed inside as the brothers exchanged a humorous glance with one another. He knew his appearance was atrocious. He also knew the O'Rifcan brothers found it amusing to make it so. But Delaney was exhausted. Country life was not for him. Though he appreciated the hospitality, he was done for the weekend. He watched as the village came into view, Claron finding a parking spot along the footpath outside a row of storefronts instead of the pub.

"Need to pop in here right quick and check on something," Riley commented.

Claron began unbuckling his seat belt, and Delaney hesitated for a split second before he realized the brothers were waiting outside the vehicle for him. He hastily unbuckled and slipped out.

Riley opened the small glass door and stepped inside to the ring of a bell. Chloe's flower shop, Delaney realized, and studied the colorful space before him. The smell of sawdust clung to perfumed air as he turned to see Chloe, Layla, and Rhea, heads bent over a catalog of some sort, and a stout redheaded man sawing through planks of wood, the noise stifling the sound of their arrival.

Chloe glanced up first and her eyes widened when they fell on him. He knew he was a sight, and the small tilt to her lips told him just how bad he looked. She tapped the catalog to snag the other women's attention. They both looked up. Rhea's face split into a pleased smile at the sight of all three of them together. Layla's blue gaze shot through Delaney as she studied him from head to toe and back up again. A laugh escaped her lips as they all began walking towards them.

"I say," Rhea cupped Claron's face in her hands and planted a welcoming kiss on his lips. "Delaney stays with you one night and you already recruit him to farm duty?" She kissed Riley's cheek and lightly tapped it as she placed a comforting hand on Delaney's shoulder. "I'm sorry, Delaney. Please excuse Claron's terrible manners."

Riley laughed and slapped Delaney on the back, which was beginning to be an annoying habit. "'Ol Del did just fine, Rhea darling. Just fine."

"It's Delaney," he grumbled through gritted teeth.

Layla looped her arm through his and walked him towards her work counter. "This be what you need, Mr. Hawkins." She rummaged through a crate of jars and bottles and plucked one out. "Here you are." She popped the lid and wafted the bottle under his nose. "A perfect fit, I wager. A little mystery in this bottle, which is perfect for you. A nice blend of black cardamom, a touch of vanilla and a wee bit of musk. Perfect for you, Mr. Hawkins." She popped the lid closed and held it up for him, her eyes level with his. "Consider it a gift. A welcome to Castlebrook gift." She urged him to take it with a nod. When his hands closed over the bottle she grinned. "Should you want more—" She reached to a small box that she had yet to open and struggled with the packing tape. "Bloody blast!" she scolded. "Conor, I need a knife."

Chloe held up her hand for a clueless Conor, as he glanced up from his work and removed the ear buds that blasted music even away from his face. "What was that? Oh, aye, if it ain't me favorite brothers." He grinned at Riley and Claron. "Sneaking up on me, are ye?"

"That I am, Conor." Riley walked towards the amiable redhead and Delaney watched as Chloe handed Layla a pair of scissors. She sliced through the tape and unfolded the tabs on the box. Slipping a business card from within, she tucked it into his shirt pocket.

"There we are, Mr. Hawkins." She winked.

"Okay," Rhea stepped forward noting Delaney's stiff posture and overwhelmed features. "Claron, take Delaney to his car, then you can come back here." She cast a pleading look to her boyfriend and Claron bit back a grin as he nodded. "Delaney, thank you for being a good sport. I hope the weather and the dairy have not ruined your opinion of Castlebrook."

Delaney cleared his throat and rolled his shoulders back. "Well, it has definitely been an... exciting 24 hours, I will say that." He rubbed his thumb over the label of the bottle in his hand. "I... I will see you Monday, Rhea."

She patted his arm in farewell.

"And thank you, Layla, for the wash." He held up the bottle.

"Don't mention it." A satisfied smile blossomed over her gorgeous face as he nodded a farewell to Chloe and followed Claron out the door towards his car.

"The poor man will never come back," Chloe whispered, and Rhea nodded in disappointed agreement.

"We'll see about that." Layla tossed her hair over her shoulder and smiled before clapping her

hands. "Come now, Rhea. We must finish our bottles." A groan escaped Rhea's lips before she could stop it and she slapped her hands over her mouth. Chloe let loose a giggle as Layla's eyes narrowed in on Rhea. "Do you not wish to help me anymore?"

"I could use some breakfast. I thought about stealing Claron and heading to the B&B for a bite. I promise I'll come back and help though." Rhea watched as Claron reached the door and entered back into the building, her entire aura glowing in his presence.

"Very well. How could I deny me older brother a chance to love on his lass?" Layla nudged Rhea towards Claron, and he caught her gently in his arms. "Go brother, woo her over breakfast. She's missed you."

Claron smiled as he bent to kiss Rhea. "You don't have to twist my arm. Come, love, let's have a quick bite." He tossed a wave towards Riley and Conor as he and Rhea walked out hand in hand and made their way up the sidewalk.

∞

She liked Sunday mornings at the B&B. It was quiet and calm, and the only sound was her mother prepping doughs and mixes for the following week at the café. And even then, her mother only worked in the mornings, so Layla

knew she would have the kitchen to herself for most of the day to finish up some of her brews, oils, and candle making. She walked through the empty café to the kitchen entrance to the B&B and walked inside. Surprise had her stopping in her tracks as Heidi Rustler stood by the oven wearing a full apron, hands resting on her hips. "As I live and breathe," Layla muttered, causing Heidi to glance up and grin.

"Well, what do you think?" She twirled and did a small jig in the apron that belonged to Sidna. "Bet you never thought this would happen."

"That I didn't." Layla continued inside, setting her crate of supplies on the island. "And why you be wearing the Mammy's apron this mornin'?"

"She's teaching me how to make her glorious bread." Heidi pulled the oven door down and peeked inside.

"'Tis not ready yet, love." Sidna bustled into the kitchen and behind the counter. "You keep openin' that door and it will never be. Letting the heat escape, you are. Must be patient." She smiled in greeting at Layla as Heidi waited impatiently at the oven. "Heidi wishes to learn the bread so as to spoil me handsome boyo."

"Are you so sure about that?" Layla pointed to Heidi as her friend stuffed a piece of bread from

Sidna's finished loaf into her mouth. Unashamedly, Heidi shrugged as the other two women laughed.

"Well, if there is any left for Riley, that is," Sidna finished.

The back door opened, and the man of the conversation entered, followed by Murphy and Tommy.

"Ah, and there he is." Sidna lifted her cheek to her sons as they each in turn placed a gentle kiss on their way to a seat. Riley paused and studied Heidi.

"Now, I say, that is a lovely sight." He walked towards her and slipped his arms around her waist and planted a slow, steamy kiss on her lips.

"Hey, watch those hands, Riley boyo," Sidna warned. "Heidi is busy. You can't swoop her away just yet."

"'Tis a right shame." Riley winked at his girl as he walked to a vacant stool beside a miserable Murphy.

"And what be wrong with you?" Sidna rubbed a comforting hand on Murphy's back as he rested his chin in his hands.

"Long night. My hopes of winning Piper over to Castlebrook have failed once again and I had to work the pub by myself last night."

"And why did you not schedule more help?" Sidna asked.

"Pride," Tommy finished for Murphy and faced his brother's scowl straight on. "Feels he can charm her to be his employee and therefore felt she would just show up last night and wish to start work immediately. Eejit."

"She said she would think about it."

"And you took that as a yes?" Layla asked. "Definitely an eejit."

Tommy harrumphed in agreement with his sister.

"Who wants to work in Galway, anyway?" Murphy asked and then pointed a quick finger at Riley. "Don't answer that."

"Give her time, love," Mrs. O'Rifcan encouraged. "Piper enjoys her work in Galway. She may not be ready to give up the city for a small village pub. Would be a big move."

"But my small pub brings in just as much as the one she works at now. She'd be paid just as handsomely."

"But she wouldn't have the city," Heidi added.

"And what be so grand about the city?" Murphy challenged.

"There's more to do," Heidi answered. "More people."

"Oh, don't bother, Heidi." Layla turned to start unpacking her supplies. "Murphy is just annoyed the lass didn't fall head over heels in love with him and agree to what he offered."

"Not true."

"Isn't it?" Layla's brows rose, and Murphy flushed at the truth to her statement.

"Alright, slightly true. I don't understand why my pub is not good enough or tempting enough to leave the one in Galway."

"Why do you wish for Piper to work for you, brother?" Riley asked.

"Because I need help and she's as smooth an operator behind the kegs as I am. She knows how to run a pub and it would give me somewhat of a break. I wouldn't have to be workin' every night of the week. Would be nice to hand over the reins to someone capable."

"And have you told her that?" Riley asked.

"Well, no. I mean, I asked her if she would like a job."

The women grunted in unison at Murphy's lack of intellect.

"What?" He innocently spread his hands completely perplexed.

"No wonder she said no." Layla shook her head in disappointment.

"For real," Heidi agreed.

Murphy straightened in his chair and looked at the women in complete and utter dismay. "And what should I have said, oh wise ones?"

Sidna held up a warning finger at his negative tone and he settled back into his slumped position, chin in hand.

"What you just said." Heidi explained. "If she knew how you viewed her work ethic and the value that would bring to you, then I think she would consider it a bit more seriously."

"Women like to know they're valued." Layla picked up from where Heidi left off. "If you just keep offering her a position in a flirtatious manner, that's all she is going to take it as. Treat her like a business asset, and she more than likely would become one, brother. Stop playing the fool as well. For you know what Heidi and I are saying is good advice."

Leaving Murphy to his thoughts, Layla turned to Riley. "You did not steal Conor away from my shelves, did you?"

"No. He is finishing them as we speak and then I will pull him away to Clary's house to take measurements."

"Another brother planning a life with a woman by his side without asking her." Layla rolled her eyes. "Clary better be certain Rhea is his before tearing up his house."

"Rhea is definitely his." Heidi confirmed.

"Aye, I just meant..." Layla wriggled her left ring finger towards Heidi and the friend nodded.

"Never wise to make drastic changes without first securing the female's opinion on the matter."

"Rhea will love the changes we plan to make." Riley, offended his sister would doubt his design abilities, stood to go about his day.

"I'm sure she will, but I imagine she would like to have her opinion listened to on the matter."

"Then that would ruin the surprise." Riley, perplexed, rested his hands on his hips to hear his sister continue.

"You boys." Heidi looked heavenward. "Are they always like this?"

Sidna nodded. "'Tis the curse of being a man."

Heidi and Layla laughed as all the brothers looked at them as if they were aliens from another planet. "Just hold off on the demolition phase until after Claron's proposal to Rhea," Heidi added.

"But I don't know when that is. I don't even think Clary knows when he will propose yet. And I've got to work his construction into me schedule." Still looking as if the entire conversation was a waste of his time, Riley shook his head and ran a hand through his hair.

"Then perhaps you should talk to your brother about this," Layla wriggled her finger again. "before talking to him about the cottage."

"Blasted women." Riley shook his head, but a smile tugged at the corners of his lips. He walked towards Heidi and planted a soft kiss to her lips. "I'll go and bother me younger brother about it right now."

"Good. Take these two as well." Sidna pointed to Tommy and Murphy. "All they be doing is lurking. Make them productive."

Neither brother offended at their mother's nagging, they stood and offered waves as they followed Riley out of the house.

"Honestly, remodeling a house when Clary hasn't even proposed yet." Layla shook her head. "Rhea will love it, no doubt, but the certainty of it without asking..."

"Rhea will love whatever they do," Sidna agreed. "But they need to be aware of opinions other than their own at times. Well done, my loves." She smiled at the two women and then clapped her hands. "And their interruption was not completely wasted. Heidi, your bread be done."

Heidi jumped to it and hustled back over to the oven and opened the door inhaling the deep and satisfying scent of baked bread. "It's perfect."

"Hurry then, butter me up a slice." Layla set aside her work so as to encourage Heidi in her baking. She would take the time to eat a piece of bread. Though the loaf was a bit misshapen, the smell was very much the same as her mother's bread, and Layla fancied a bite. "Nothing quite like the taste of fresh baked bread."

Heidi, pleased that her bread was being well-received, set about slicing it up. She handed Sidna and Layla a slice while she cut her own. Sidna studied it from every angle as if measuring it for a baking competition. She then took a bite, Heidi's eyes hopeful as she watched.

"Lovely." Sidna smiled, pleased with her student.

Layla's teeth sank into the airy slice and she nodded. "That'll do, Rustler, that'll do."

Heidi beamed. "I think I could make a million more and it would never be enough."

Laughing, Sidna patted her arm. "You can prep the loaves for supper tonight."

Receiving the honor of making a dish for the family meal did not go unnoticed as Layla and Heidi both stood in complete surprise at Mrs. O'Rifcan's offer.

"For now, Heidi, we should allow Layla use of the kitchen. Unless you plan to help her?"

"I was actually going to spend some time with Riley this afternoon." She looked at Layla regrettably.

"Not to worry, Heidi." Layla smiled. "Rhea be wandering in shortly to help. Chloe as well. On with ye. Me brother needs your wise counsel. Perhaps you can share some wisdom with Clary while you're over there." She winked at Heidi as her friend untied the apron and hung it on the same hook as the others that awaited fellow café workers. "Have a care." Layla waved at her as she exited.

"Does a Mammy's heart good to see her sons finding loves." Sidna's soft smile had Layla

wrapping an arm around her shoulders in a tight squeeze.

"They be good for them, that is for certain."

"Now if they'd only hurry it up so I can have some more grands, that would be quite fine by me too."

Layla laughed. "One step at a time, Mam. One step at a time."

"Wouldn't hurt you to be thinking of the future as well. Yes, the business is quite right for ye, but a love would be as well."

Layla cringed. Her mother never passed up an opportunity to discuss dating or love. And though she enjoyed her dating life, normally, Layla continually reminded herself that her time and energy needed to focus upon her new business. For now. Once it was up and running, perhaps then she could return to her lush dating field. And though she didn't quite understand it, nor appreciate it, Delaney Hawkins' face emerged in her thoughts and settled there. She kept her hands busy, setting wicks in jars as her mother quietly exited the kitchen. "Focus now, Layla," she murmured to herself. "No need to think of the grumpy Welshman. No need a'tall." Unconvinced, her brain decided to remind her of his frumpy, unkempt, dairy-infused appearance from the day before and a smile tugged at her lips as she worked in contented silence.

«CHAPTER FIVE»

Delaney knew the moment Rhea entered his office. She had a certain perfume that wafted before and after her everywhere she went lately. It was a pleasing scent, soft and floral. Delicate. Much the way he would describe Rhea, though the delicate description was in question after experiencing the dairy work this past weekend. If Rhea could handle that, she was certainly not delicate. He looked up and smiled.

"So, I finished the Edmondson's file." She placed it on his desk and sat in one of the free chairs across from his desk. She sniffed. "Are you wearing cologne?"

He balked at her boldness to ask him such a question. However, for some reason, Rhea's lack of professionalism did not bother him as much as he thought it would. *Were they becoming friends,* he wondered. He cleared his throat and flipped open her file. "No. I am not." Hoping she would leave it at that, he perused her work.

"Something's different." She sniffed again, leaning closer to his desk. "I know that smell." *Sniff. Sniff.*

He sighed and leaned back in his chair, uncomfortable. She giggled. "You used Layla's shower wash."

"I did."

"I thought I recognized the smell. It's a good scent for you."

Feeling awkward at her fowardness, Delaney looked back down at the folder. "Thank you."

"She does offer it in a cologne as well. Want me to bring you a bottle next week? I can grab it this weekend."

"That is unnecessary. I do not wear cologne."

"That's a shame. It's a great scent for you."

"Can we focus on the file, please?" He pointed at the papers and Rhea clapped her hands.

"Yes. Of course. So, I laid out their expenses in a separate spreadsheet for each property, breaking it down that way instead of all together. To be honest, they took a hit this year on that third piece of property. But—" She shrugged.

"Thank you, Rhea. I'll submit it today."

She stood at his dismissal. "I'll be going to lunch with Heidi at noon. You should join us."

Delaney looked up, his dark eyes searching her face to gauge her seriousness. Rhea fisted her hands on her hips. "Only if you want to. No pressure. Just giving you an opportunity to get out of this stuffy office."

"I would be glad to join you."

A smile spread over her face. "Good. We'll wait for you at the elevator." She hurried off down the hall back towards her office.

He leaned back in his chair and sighed, running his hands over his face. Why? Why did he agree to lunch with his co-workers? He never did that. He never wanted to. So why? Why did he wish to spend more time with Rhea and Heidi? Inwardly he knew the answer was that he wished to belong, and that his time in Castlebrook had only made him wish to have a family atmosphere like the O'Rifcans. But, ever the controlled one, Delaney nudged those thoughts away and

considered himself just confused and perplexed over the matter. Longings were for the faint hearted, not for him. He was a successful man. *Happy*? He pondered that a moment. *Somewhat happy*, he amended. He didn't need a large family or— he thought of Riley's annoying habits of slapping him on the back and calling him Del. He cringed. He did not enjoy that, at all. Resolute that his whimsical thoughts about a family of his own were preposterous, he transferred his office phone extension to the secretary out front. Lunch with his co-workers awaited him, and he chastised himself for his eagerness. He tampered down the pleasure and locked his office. He'd eat and chat about whatever the two women wished and appear to enjoy himself. However, he affirmed his decision that he would not accept any future invitations. Keep business and personal separate. It was his way. And he didn't need Rhea and Heidi disrupting his carefully controlled and structured life.

He forced a polite smile as Rhea and Heidi awaited him in the lobby. Rhea pressed the button on the elevator. "Sandwich and soup?" She asked him.

"Sounds fine."

Heidi stepped into the vacant elevator cart and eyed Rhea in amusement as Delaney stood stiff-backed in front of them. They walked towards

the east side of the office building's first floor and into a food court of multiple restaurants and cafes. A small sandwich shop sat in the corner and Rhea hurried over to step in line. She ordered, followed by Heidi. "We'll go grab a seat," she told him, pointing towards the wall of windows that overlooked the bustling streets. He nodded and ordered his usual roast beef sandwich and tomato bisque.

When he accepted his receipt, he turned and found the familiar eyes of Layla O'Rifcan. She flashed a gorgeous smile and reached to squeeze his arm. "Mr. Hawkins, what a pleasant surprise." She leaned forward and lightly brushed her lips over his cheek. He caught the interested stare of the man behind her as his eyes wandered up and down Layla. The O'Rifcan sister was oblivious to the attention.

"Nice to see you, Layla." He stepped out of the way so she could move forward in line and order.

"Don't run away just yet, Mr. Hawkins. I wish to speak with you." She grinned as she then turned her attention to the worker before her. When she collected her change and receipt, she slipped her arm through his and began walking towards Rhea and Heidi. "I'm here to join the girls for lunch. I did not realize you would be joining us." She leaned closer to him and lightly sniffed. He jerked at the intimacy and she laughed. "You will have to excuse

me, Mr. Hawkins. I am a woman of interest when it comes to scents. But I believe the one I am smelling is one of mine. You used me wash." Pleasure lit her sparkling blue eyes. "And how do you find it?"

"It's nice. Thank you."

"Just nice?" she prodded.

"Not overpowering," he added.

"Well, we certainly couldn't have that, could we?"

They reached the table and Layla winked at Rhea in greeting as Delaney waited for Layla to sit before taking his own seat. "Bumped into your Mr. Hawkins, Rhea. I'm pleased to see you've dragged him out of his burrow."

Ignoring their banter, Delaney fidgeted with a napkin as he unrolled his silverware.

"You know, Mr. Hawkins," Layla continued.

"It's Delaney. You do not have to call me Mr. Hawkins."

"Ah, well that's a lovely thing, isn't it?" Layla beamed. "I happen to like Mr. Hawkins. Suits you. All polished and refined." She lightly tugged on his tie which had him instinctively shifting away from her. "Oh come now, Delaney," she teased.

His name sounded slightly musical on her lips. Different. Not the usual way he'd heard it. Certainly not in the Americanized accents of Rhea and Heidi. With Layla, it rolled off her tongue with a touch of Irish brogue combined with sensualism. Which, he concluded, was an exact description of the woman herself. "You know, I have some cologne to match that wash." Layla nodded towards him as their food was placed before them.

"I already tried to convince him," Rhea chimed in. "He didn't want any."

Feigning offense, Layla held her hand to her heart. "And why not?"

"He doesn't wear cologne."

"I am right here, thank you," Delaney muttered through clenched teeth. He despised being talked about as though he weren't present.

Layla smirked. "You wouldn't wear it if I gave you some?" she asked, her lush lashes slightly covering her blue gaze.

"I do not wear cologne," he repeated.

"Ah, but how could you turn down a gift?"

"Why would you wish to give me some?" he countered and met her gaze head on.

"Because I consider you a challenge. If I can get the industrious Mr. Delaney Hawkins to use and wear my products, why, I imagine I could get just about anyone to do so." She grinned and slightly brushed her fingertip over the dimple in his chin.

Astounded, Delaney turned towards his food and began eating. Rhea cast Layla a warning look to tone down her flirtation. Layla shrugged.

"Oh, Rhea, I almost forgot. Roland wishes for you to join him Wednesday at his flat for a meal. Said it's been too long since you and Clary came by to eat with just him."

"I'm afraid that's true. We used to eat there every Saturday, but we've been sort of doing our own thing for quite a while since weekends are our only time together. I'll make sure of it. Tell him I will be there."

"Will do. He'll be pleased." Layla spooned a sip of her soup. "He be a good date, that Roland."

"Is that so?" Rhea laughed as she eyed her friend.

"He is. Met him at McCarthy's Restaurant the other day for a dinner. Treated me to one of Conor's famous pizzas."

"Thank you." Rhea held a hand to her heart. "For seeing about him while I'm not there."

"Was not seeing about him. Was pure selfishness on my part, wanting a dinner with a handsome man." Layla waved away Rhea's guilt with a flick of her hand.

"Roland is your grandfather, correct?" Delaney asked.

"Yes."

He nodded as if he was now fully caught up with the conversation.

"I don't know how Conor is managing so much work lately," Heidi added. "The shop and then working at his family's restaurant. He's a trooper."

"No doubt about that," Layla added. "He's an angel for sure and certain. My shelves look glorious. They be drying for the rest of today and then tomorrow I can start placing products."

"That's exciting!" Rhea cheered. "I can't wait for the grand opening. Oh!" She turned excited eyes towards Delaney. "You should come, Delaney."

He wasn't quite sure how to respond. Layla leaned towards him and popped a crisp into her mouth awaiting his response, amused that he was so uncomfortable by the invitation.

"When is it?" he asked.

"Would be two weeks' time," Layla stated. "Not this Saturday, but the next."

He nodded.

"So, is that a yes?" Rhea asked. "Will you come?"

"I will have to check my schedule. But thank you for the invitation."

"Oh, Mr. Hawkins, you have to come. You're one of my guinea pigs. People need to see a success story. A man who never cared what products he's used and is now a loyal customer."

"I haven't bought anything," he pointed out, making her laugh.

"Oh, but you will." She patted his hand as if he were a simpleton. "Would be quite helpful to have a customer there that is not one of me brothers. Other clientele might purchase seeing that as well."

"I'll consider it." He hoped that answer would suffice.

She grinned. "I will mark you down then."

"I said I would consider it, not that I would come."

"Oh, you will come." Layla's assurance perplexed him.

"You're a confident one, aren't you?" he asked.

"Yes." She looked to the other women as they all nodded.

Shaking his head, the women chuckled as he avoided further discussion on the topic. He wasn't so sure he would be going, but when Layla looked at him as if he were the only man in the room, he felt his heart wish to say yes. She was a dangerous one, and he felt that, despite his best efforts, he may just fall into her trap.

∞

Layla adjusted the vanilla scented candle just a smidgen and fluffed the lavender that nestled around it inside the woven basket. Perfect. She stepped back, admiring the freshly stained shelves and what little product she'd organized and merchandised on the shelves. No doubt this would be her favorite task to complete in her new shop. Placing her own products on her own shelves pleased her. So much so, that she'd spent half the morning completing just two small displays. It had to be perfect. Every petal, candle, sachet, lotion, cream, or wash had to be expertly placed.

She reached into the crate at her feet and retrieved her rose collection. Heidi's signature scent. She chuckled at the thought of Heidi hoarding the products before she'd flown back to Texas. Little did Rustler know she would be heading right back to Ireland a few weeks later

and would have fresh inventory to choose from. Fate had a sense of humor sometimes. Or was it destiny? Either way, Heidi Rustler was meant to be with her brother, Riley. And though it took Layla a while to warm up to the brash Texan, she now considered Heidi a dear friend. She scattered dried rose petals around the bottles, thankful that Chloe let her have the spare petals that seemed to find their way to the floors ever so often. She stepped back to survey her work and nodded in approval. She still had quite a bit of shelf space to fill, along with two free-standing display stands that needed product. With that in mind, she walked back over to her work counter—her *glorious* work counter. She smoothed a hand down the glossy wood and a thrill seeped into her veins. The thrill that comes from the touch of luxury and ownership. Conor, the genius, had created beauty for her. Sheer beauty.

She reached into one of her new cabinets and retrieved a large metal mixing bowl. She then reached by her feet and lifted an oversized bag of hydrated magnesium sulfate and scooped three large scoops into the bowl. She then bent down to retrieve a bag of sea salt and generously scooped a portion into the bowl as well. She slowly stirred them together with a wooden spoon then reached over to check the bundle of flowers she had drying on the counter. She'd rinsed them the day before and dried their petals, and they'd dried perfectly for her to grind them down and mix them into the

salts. The delicate petal was soft to the touch, but desiccated. Daisies. Rhea did not realize she'd given Layla the idea of the scent, so once Rhea smelled it, she would know it was hers. Rhea always claimed Clary smelled of sunshine. That thought had Layla smiling, because it was true. Her brother carried the scent of the outdoors with him everywhere he went. Though it was sometimes masked by the scent of cow manure, the underlying freshness was always there. Now, Rhea needed a scent to match. She pressed a finger against the dried lemon peels and strawberries she'd had dehydrated over the weekend. Their scents were contained inside the small bottle, that when opened, flooded the entire room. Something was missing, and as her eyes wandered over the various drying flowers around her, she spotted the missing ingredient. Honeysuckle. She retrieved several sprigs and plucked a few of the daisies and tossed them into her mortar. Daisies, honeysuckle, lemon, strawberry. Yes, bottling sunshine was a task, but based on the smells wafting from her mortar, Layla knew she'd done it. Rhea in a bottle. Light, bright, and a touch of sweet. Her friend would love it. And so would Clary.

The bell above the door jingled and Layla looked up to find her sister, Lorena, walking inside with an unfamiliar frown marring her otherwise wrinkle-free forehead. Her older sister was like a willow tree: tall, strong, but soft and graceful in movement. She signified strength and beauty, and

as the oldest of the O'Rifcan children, Lorena had needed that strength over the years. Her face held a perfect mixture of their mammy and their da and a touch of every sibling. Her eyes, the same blue as Layla's, her hair a mixture of browns and blonde streaks had her resembling Murphy and Clary now and again. But the wide smile she shared with Declan. The high cheekbones with Chloe, and her easygoing nature could be mirrored by Riley, Tommy, or Jace depending on which brother shared a space with her at the time. Jaron, ah... he was carried in the very frown etched across Lorena's forehead. The same wrinkle and concerned expression that fluttered over Jaron's face now and again currently tarnished Lorena's normally cheerful disposition.

"Sister." She laid her purse on the counter and slipped onto a stool facing Layla.

"And what brings you by, Rena?"

"I believe I am quite possibly the worst mammy in the world."

"Oh, well I highly doubt that." Layla smirked and continued grinding the pestle into the mortar. "Tell me what has you acting the maggot, sister."

"'Tis Rose."

Thinking of her little niece, Layla smiled. "And is Rosie fine then?"

"Aye, she be fine. Just turning six is all, and demanding a party fit for a queen."

Layla laughed and that caused Lorena's frown to slowly disappear as she, too, relaxed and smiled at the notions of her spritely daughter.

"I just haven't had the time to think, much less plan, a party yet. And her birthday be Friday."

"Rosie would be fine with a fun tea of some sort. Simple."

"Normally, yes, she would. However, I believe she's taken a liking to Heidi as of late and wishes to make her opinions known... louder than usual."

Again, Layla laughed. "Aye, Rustler has an opinion of things and is not afraid to voice them."

"Would I be placing too much on you, sister, if I asked for your help in the plannin'?" Lorena asked.

Layla shook her head. "Not a'tall. I would love to help."

"You're a lifesaver."

Layla walked towards a shelf and plucked a small bottle and uncapped it. She grabbed Lorena's hand and squirted a small portion into her palm. Lorena sniffed and then began to lather it into her skin. "Oh, well now that's lovely."

"'Will be good for your hands. All the dishes you wash for Mam is hard on the skin."

"Aye, that is true enough." Lorena finished lathering her hands and held them to her nose. "This be so divine."

"'Tis your scent. Jasmine, violets, lavender, and a wee touch of musk. When I made it, I thought of you, Rena. So, 'tis your scent."

"That's a sweet thought. Thank you." Lorena reached across the counter and squeezed Layla's hand before standing and shouldering her purse. She picked up the small bottle and held it over her open bag. "Sample? Or shall I pay?"

"A free sample." Layla grinned.

Lorena plopped the bottle in her bag. "I feel like I smell quite luxurious now."

"As you should."

Lorena walked to the door. "I will let you know when Rosie decides between fairies and unicorns for her party."

"Tough decision there. I shall be waiting on pins and needles."

Laughing, Lorena waved farewell as she exited.

Contented, Layla sighed and went back to her mixture. She poured the petals in with the salts and then placed lemon peels and strawberries into the mix as well and stirred to combine it. Her cell phone jingled and she swiped to answer. "This be Layla." She listened as a baritone voice requested a night out and a bit of fun afterwards. Benjamin. Layla wracked her brain trying to envision a face to go with the name, but her mind came up empty. *Must not have made an impression*, she thought.

"Terribly sorry, Benjamin, but I'm opening a business see, and I'm very—" A click sounded in her ear as he hung up without even listening to her full reply. Offended, Layla stared at her phone in shock. "Eejit," she muttered, tossing the phone onto the counter. How dare he call just to see if she would be a whimsy for the night. Is that all he thought of her? Apparently. She shuddered, thankful she dodged a man like that. But then worry set in. Is that how most people saw her? Is that how men saw her? Good for a bit of fun and that was it? And if they saw her as a no good doxie, what did the female population think? She knew she shouldered a bit of dislike at the pub here and there, but was it enough bad blood to hurt her chances of succeeding at her business? She worried her bottom lip as she surveyed her work space once more, this time with a regretful eye. There's no way she could fail. She was so in love with the idea of her own space. Her own path. She couldn't possibly give it up now or later. But if she

faced off against a soured reputation then her hopes would slowly dwindle.

She slapped a hand on the counter and reached for her purse. "Well, I won't be having any more of this mood," she decided. She quickly stored the salt mixture into a sealable container and set it on a shelf, slipping her purse onto her shoulder. She needed a wee bit of encouragement. Empowerment that could only come from one female in particular. Rhea. As she fished for her keys, Layla darted towards her little red sports car and slid inside. She was off to Limerick.

«CHAPTER SIX»

Delaney pressed a button on his receiver and set his phone in its cradle to speak to Rhea on speaker. Though she was just down the hall, sometimes, so as not to interrupt complete work flow, they'd just communicate via phone. "I'm telling you, Delaney, it's just not adding up for me. I'll run through the numbers again. But this is the fifth time. If they do not add up again, then we are officially missing something."

Grunting, Delaney eyed the screen in front of him. He scrolled through the files Rhea had sent him to look at. "It looks like it is all there, Rhea. But yes, run through it once more. Fresh. From the beginning. Not just the current forms you're looking at." He knew she would not like that

answer, but she only sighed. "Sure thing, Delaney." The secretary's voice filtered through the line as she stood in Rhea's office. "Rhea, there's a Layla O'Rifcan here to see you."

"Layla?" Rhea asked.

"Yes ma'am."

"Alright, I'll be right out." He heard her shuffling papers on her desk. "Sorry, Delaney, apparently Layla is here for some reason. I'll get this file done before the end of the day, even if I have to work through lunch."

"Sounds like a plan, Rhea. Thank you for being diligent."

She hung up and he heard the sounds of feminine chatter down the hall. From the sounds of it, Rhea was not expecting Layla to stop by. He wondered what brought the sister to Rhea's work, of all places. It was hardly the place for friendly banter, especially during business hours. He knew Rhea would work late to make up her time, but still, Delaney couldn't fathom why Layla thought it would be okay to venture into the office now. Curious, he stood to his feet and walked towards his office door and cracked it open.

"Can you believe it?" Layla's voice, full of anger, had him leaning further out the door in response. He saw Heidi poke her head out of her door as

well. Their eyes met and he immediately regretted his eavesdropping. She mouthed, "Layla?", towards him and he nodded. Concern etched her face as she slipped back into her office. Though she was Layla's friend, even Heidi seemed to know when to avoid the sister. Delaney, however, felt a tug to venture closer towards her. It was his office after all. He should be free to walk wherever he pleased. His feet took on a mind of their own as they headed towards Rhea's office. The door was mostly closed but cracked just enough that he heard a sniffle and Rhea's quiet voice soothing a ruffled Layla.

"I don't see why you're letting one faceless man ruin your day, Layla. Clearly, he did not make a solid impression on you in the first place, so I would not give his reaction a fraction of a thought. You know who you are and so does everyone else. Don't let that one silly phone call make you question all the hard work you've been doing in preparation for your grand opening."

"But don't you see?" Layla continued. "If he thinks that, do others?"

"I think you're reading way too much into this. And I think it is just your nerves talking."

"It's haunted me all morning, and on the drive over," Layla admitted. "I feel completely deflated."

"And you shouldn't," Rhea stated with an air of finality. "More people like you than dislike you, Layla. And that's not counting all the new faces and customers that will be shopping with you as well. I mean, look at Delaney. He is a perfect example."

"According to him, he is not officially my customer yet," Layla grumbled.

"He will be," Rhea encouraged. "You gave him that wash, and he's smelled like it every day since. I guarantee you he will be a repeat customer." Smiling, Rhea straightened a stack of papers on her desk. "There will be more like him. You have a way with people, Layla. You can make them feel special, and the attention you give in pairing someone with the right product will only help your business grow. Do not let this man's opinion of you, or lack thereof, change your goal."

"I knew I needed to see you." Layla sniffled and laughed as Rhea smiled. "I'm glad I could help."

"Would you like to go to lunch?"

"I wish I could, but Delaney has me checking over a file. Unfortunately, I can't seem to find what's missing, and I have a feeling it's going to take me the rest of the day and part of the evening to find it. My hopes of dinner with Grandpa and Claron tonight are slowly dwindling."

"Surely he won't make you stay late when you have plans."

"If I can't solve this mystery, I need to."

"Preposterous. You will leave at closing time, Rhea. Roland has missed you. Mr. Hawkins will just have to wait for you to finish the file tomorrow."

A chuckle escaped Rhea's lips. "That's not quite how it works here, Layla. But I'm going to do my best to get it done."

Delaney shifted on his feet. Apparently, his reputation was that of a stubborn and bossy mule. It's not that he wished for Rhea to have to work late. He just knew that, other than himself, she was the best at fixing issues in problem files. Would it hurt for him to look over the file? Perhaps a pair of fresh eyes is what it needed. Rhea had already combed through it four times. Was he being a jerk to ask her to do it again? He didn't realize she had dinner plans this evening. Well, now that he thought about it, maybe he did. He'd heard the conversation about Wednesday with Roland, it just slipped his mind. And Rhea hadn't mentioned it to him. Though he could sense her reluctance over running through the file from start to finish again, he hadn't realized it was because she'd wished to drive to Castlebrook this evening. She'd simply agreed. He tapped his knuckles on her door frame and opened the door. He pretended to be surprised by Layla's presence.

"Oh, terribly sorry, Rhea. I didn't realize you still had a visitor." Layla quickly diverted her gaze and he noticed her trying to swipe away the remainder of her tears. Rhea's lie detector signal flared as she studied him. He flushed, realizing he was found out. "I, um, was coming to retrieve the Matson file from you."

"But I'm working on it. I'm not finished running through it again."

"I know." He stepped forward and nodded for her to start shuffling the papers back into the folder. "I thought it might be best for a pair of fresh eyes to take a look at it. Maybe you've looked at it a bit too much."

Surprise had Rhea's movements halting as she openly gaped at him. "You don't want me to do it?"

Trying to appear nonchalant, Delaney waved away her worry. "No, I'll take care of it. I'd rather have you moving on to a new one."

"If I start a new one now, I will only get the organization charts set up. I won't be able to start digging into it until tomorrow."

"That's fine, then," Delaney motioned for her to hand the folder over. Confusion still omnipresent over Rhea's face, he smiled reassuringly. "Come now, Rhea. I haven't all day."

"I just... don't understand. But if you want it, here you go." She handed it to him.

"Why don't you take a breather. Go get some lunch, come back and then start work on the next file?" Delaney motioned towards Layla with his head, the sister still avoiding eye contact. "I'm sure Layla would stick around to eat with you. Right, Layla?"

The sister nodded and cleared her throat. "Yes, of course. I would love for you to eat with me, Rhea." She forced a polite smile Delaney's way and his gut twisted at the miserable expression in Layla's eyes. Whatever man had caused such torment, he wished to punch him in the face. Surprised by his own sudden instinct, he turned back to Rhea's dumbfounded expression. "Ah, okay. Sure. I will go to lunch. Did you— would you want to come?" she awkwardly invited, and he smirked.

"No, thanks. My plan is to peruse this for the next six hours or so." He held up the file as Rhea gathered her purse and stood. She motioned for Layla to do the same.

"I can bring you something back," she offered.

He just shook his head. "No need, but thanks. You two have a nice meal. Layla, it was a pleasure." He nodded as Layla walked by him and towards the lobby. Rhea paused briefly and placed a hand on his arm and squeezed. "Thank you,

Delaney," she whispered. "Thank you for letting me be there for her." Without waiting for a response, Rhea walked away and left him dreading the folder in his hand. It was going to be another long night at the office for him, but knowing Layla received the attention she needed from Rhea didn't make the extra work seem so bad. He hoped.

∞

It was just what she needed, a lunch with Rhea, and she was disappointed it couldn't last longer. But Rhea's work needed to be done. Though by a surprising twist, Mr. Hawkins had offered to take part of her work load, Layla knew Rhea still needed to get back to her office. She decided to hand deliver the cheesecake she'd ordered for Rhea's boss as a thank you for lending Rhea to her for the last hour. She tapped her knuckles on Delaney's door and she heard a muffled, "Come in." When she opened it, his back was to her as he had one hand tangled in the mop of wavy curls on top of his head and the other holding the phone to his ear. He swiveled around in his chair and his eyes widened in surprise. "I'll call you back," he mumbled and hung up the receiver. "Layla. I wasn't expecting you." He straightened in his chair and readjusted his glasses as she walked inside. She placed the boxed delicacy on his desk. "A thank you, Mr. Hawkins, for letting me steal Rhea away for the lunch hour."

"Oh, well it was no trouble."

"Yes, 'twas. And I appreciate it. I had a wee rough patch to work through and Rhea helped. So, thank you." She motioned towards the cheesecake.

"Then you're welcome. I'm glad Rhea was able to…" He wasn't quite sure what to say. Pleasantries were always awkward for him. He fumbled a moment and Layla stifled a giggle. "Oh, come now, Mr. Hawkins, you can do it," she encouraged.

He blushed but a slow smile spread over his face and he shook his head. "I apologize for my awkwardness, Layla, I'm a bit new to…"

"Caring?" she asked.

A brief look of disappointment washed over his face before he replaced it with a forced smile. "I was going to say interaction."

"Ah." She smirked. "Well, perhaps you should have more practice, Mr. Hawkins. In a week and a half, I will expect you to be at my grand opening. Perfect place for mingling and interacting."

"I have it on my calendar, should I be available."

"Oh, do you now? Penciled in, am I? And where is this calendar of yours?" she asked.

He pointed to the large desk calendar spread out on a table nearest the window. Layla

walked towards him and plucked the pen from his shirt pocket and stalked over to the calendar. He stood, instinctively, as if she were going to steal something, and followed her. She leaned down and found the corresponding date and traced over his writing in permanent ink. *"Layla O'Rifcan – Grand Opening – Castlebrook."* She then added a small notation underneath it. *"Attend or face the consequences."* When she finished, she leaned up with a challenging glimmer in her eyes. She slipped his pen back into his pocket. "Now it is confirmed. So glad you can make it, Mr. Hawkins. 'Twill be a perfect opportunity for you to purchase more of that wash you seem to be so fond of." She winked as she walked towards his office door.

He patted his pocket where the pen settled. "I, ah..." He fumbled with what to say and her smile only broadened. "You do not have to call me, Mr. Hawkins. I've told you that already."

Her brow quirked a moment. "Good day to you, Mr. Hawkins." She walked out and left him grinding his teeth in frustration. Pleased, Layla liked that she could ruffle Delaney's feathers a bit. She punched the button to the elevator and waited. The secretary glanced up as Delaney walked into the lobby and headed straight for Layla. She inhaled a sharp breath as the doors to the elevator opened and he slipped in right before they closed again. His eyes were sharp and he slipped his glasses off, shoulders back and that arrogant chin tilted ever

so slightly. "My name is Delaney. Not Del, nor Mr. Hawkins. I would appreciate if you O'Rifcans would just simply say it as it is. And second, I do not respond kindly to threats."

"Since when did I threaten you?"

"Attend or face the consequences? You literally just wrote that on my calendar."

"Ah. I did, didn't I?"

"And third. I do not appreciate being bossed around like some... some school boy. *If* I am free that Friday, I will come to your shop's opening. If I am not, I will not."

"Of course." Amused that he'd felt the need to assert himself, Layla leaned against the wall of the elevator and waited patiently for him to continue. His dark eyes honed in on her like a hawk and she found this suddenly irate version of Delaney immensely attractive. As he rambled on about demands and "lack of formality," Layla waited.

"And why, for bloody's sake, have the doors not opened yet?" he motioned towards the elevator and Layla laughed.

She slipped towards him and reached behind him, firmly pressing the button that would take them down to the first floor. "That ought to get us moving," she whispered. She did not move

away from him as they slowly drifted downward. Inches from him, she stood tall. She liked that even though she was wearing high heels, she still had to look up just a notch to meet those angry and frustrated eyes of his. When the elevator glided to a halt and the doors swished open, several people began to enter. Layla leaned forward and lightly brushed her lips over his cheek. "I'll be seeing you, Delaney," she whispered. She then slipped out before he could catch a single breath. She caught his reflection in the glass windows opposite the elevator and smiled to herself as sheer annoyance radiated from him. As she hopped into her car and looked up at the building she'd just exited, Layla had the sudden realization that Delaney Hawkins had just stolen a piece of her heart. Surprisingly content with that thought, she turned the key and set out towards home.

«CHAPTER SEVEN»

He wasn't sure why he'd accepted Rhea's invitation to Castlebrook for the weekend. He was still overcoming the horrors of the previous weekend that he'd visited the place. But her reasoning was sound. Claron had hoped to have some men over while his niece's birthday party was happening at his house. Surrounded by women and little girls could easily drive a man mad, so Delaney felt, as a fellow man, it was his duty to help a friend out. *Friend? Was Claron his friend?* He still wasn't quite sure of that yet, but he felt like perhaps they could be—or already were— he just didn't know how it all worked, but he was content with trying to be more sociable. Maybe. Rhea had implored him on behalf of her boyfriend, saying that Claron hardly had friends outside of

his brothers and that it would be good for him to have someone from the outside to hang out with now and again. Either Rhea was full of it, or Claron was in much the same boat as Delaney. All work and no play, and therefore, not a large list of friends to call upon when he wanted.

He topped the hill of Angel's Gap and parked his car next to a small red sports car in a long line of other vehicles. Festivities seemed to flow in and out of the small cottage and pink and purple tassels hung alongside paper lanterns of the same shades all around the quaint flower garden in front. Little girls dressed in fairy wings ran to and fro, laughing and giggling as they threw glitter at one another. If he ever doubted that Claron O'Rifcan was a good man, he needn't any longer. Delaney quickly elevated him to sainthood as he walked towards the side patio that overlooked the Gap while shrill screams of pure joy echoed all around. He found the adults scattered about, and Rhea caught his eye and waved, walking towards him. She tapped Claron on the back as she passed him, and her boyfriend jumped to attention quickly.

"I'm so glad you could make it." She smiled in welcome.

"I wasn't sure if I was to bring a gift or not," Delaney admitted.

Rhea shook her head. "No, trust me, Rose has more than enough." She motioned towards a table piled high with gifts, dressed in perfectly tied ribbons in the many colors of the rainbow and all things purely little girl. Claron stepped forward and extended his hand. "I appreciate you coming to add to the testosterone level around here."

Delaney smiled as Claron handed him a fresh beer. "Come, the men be this way. We have to clearly establish this side of the overhanging so as to confirm we are not fairies or unicorns."

Riley nodded in greeting as Delaney walked up. "Del, good to see you."

He let the nickname slide, tapping his bottle against a seated Murphy's in greeting as the blond-headed brother sat on a wooden stool near a hot grill.

"Did you get your wings?" Murphy asked, pointing to the too small, glitter-dusted wings strapped to his back.

"Is it a requirement?" Delaney asked, amused.

"That would be a no. Well, unless you're the favorite uncle," Murphy explained.

"Second favorite," Claron clarified. "I be Rosie's number one."

"'Tis truth to that," Murphy admitted. "This be my way of trying to sneak past him in the ranks."

Murphy took a long swig of his beer as Riley ventured away and a little girl with brown curls bounced in front of Delaney.

"Hello there. I'm Rose. I don't know you. It's my birthday," she said boldly.

Delaney could not help but grin at the cute girl, her blue eyes shining up at him as she waited for his response.

"My name is Delaney. It is nice to meet you, Rose. Best of birthdays to you."

"Are you a friend to me uncles?" She asked, lightly shifting from one foot to the other as energy radiated from her petite frame.

"More of an acquaintance," Delaney clarified and inwardly kicked himself as he saw confusion furrow the little girl's brow and her head tilted to the side.

"What's that?" she asked. "They be grand, once you get to know them."

Claron and Murphy laughed as the former reached over, tugged one of her curls and winked at her.

"I'm sure they are."

"You don't want to be their friend?" she continued.

"Oh, it's not that, I—"

"Rosie," Layla's voice called to the small girl as she walked up and slipped her arm through Delaney's. "Don't be bothering Mr. Hawkins with a thousand questions. Go have fun with your friends. They wish to flutter about in their new wings."

Rose's keen eyes bounced between Layla and Delaney. "So, he is your friend?" she asked.

"Aye. Now go." Layla waved her away.

"But you promised to fly with us," Rose reminded her.

"Aye. And I will once I've said a proper hello to Mr. Hawkins. Now, on with ye." Rose turned and skipped a few hops before turning again.

"Thanks for coming to me party, Mr. Delaney. I like you." She bounced away in an energetic burst that turned into squeals of pure pleasure as she raced around with her friends.

"That's an enthusiastic birthday girl," Delaney commented.

"Aye, she is," Claron confirmed. "Our darling little Rose."

"Rhea speaks of her often. I somehow envisioned a shy little lass, but it would seem she takes after you." Delaney turned towards Layla.

"Does she now?" Layla quirked her head in much the same way Rose had, and his lips twitched as the brothers noticed the same resemblance in the movement. "I don't know... she does love Rhea."

"Who doesn't?" Murphy replied and toasted towards an amused Claron. "But Rosie does love her aunts. Especially an aunt who throws her an epic party."

"Perhaps you're right." Layla grinned. "Now, where did Riley run off to? He was to fetch more lemonade."

"In the house, I believe." Claron pointed towards the door as he went back to his grill and turned several pieces of roasting meat. It smelled heavenly.

"Come Delaney, let me show you about." Layla tugged on his arm and he reluctantly followed.

"Seems a large crowd for a little girl's birthday," he commented quietly.

"Ah, but don't you know we O'Rifcans love to throw a party?" Layla chuckled as she pointed towards a small group of people. "Those be the parents of the other children, and of course, my

sister, Lorena, and her husband, Paul, Rose's parents. And me Mammy talking their heads off." Layla waved as her mother spotted them, a large smile blossoming on her face at seeing Layla and Delaney arm in arm. "Hurry and avert your eyes, Mr. Hawkins, or me mother will swoop in and corner you for conversation."

He did not have to be told twice.

"There be Heidi with Piper. She's a friend from Galway, helps Murphy at the pub now and again. He's attempting to woo her to Castlebrook to work for him, but has yet to succeed." Delaney studied the short blonde woman and watched as she and Heidi burst into laughter mid conversation. They looked like old friends.

"Let's see... most of me brothers you met at the meal the other night, but Tommy has his lass with him, Denise." She pointed to the redheaded brother and sandy haired woman that stood next to him. A *decent looking couple,* he mused.

"And of course, our Rhea and Clary. They can only go about five minutes away from one another and then one of them has to circle back around and steal a kiss. 'Tis quite sweet to see me brother act a fool. Ah, and there's Conor." She waved, and the man toasted towards her in response before turning back to his conversation with a reappearing Riley. "I see Riley is avoiding his lemonade duties. They be plotting over their next

project, I'm sure," she added. "And then there's Rosie and all her friends." She pointed to a train of young girls pretending to fly through the meadow. Chloe, the youngest O'Rifcan sister, ran with them. All carried ribbon sticks and beautiful rainbows of colored streamers blew behind them as they ran.

"Your sister looks the part of fairy very well." He nodded in Chloe's direction and Layla smiled.

"Aye. We always say Chloe is gifted by the fairies. Her talent for flowers and such."

"And you, no doubt, with all your concoctions."

"That be a nice thing to say." Layla turned to him pleased. "And odd, coming from you."

"Why is that odd?" he asked, lightly nudging his glasses up his nose as they continued walking about the garden.

She narrowed her eyes and studied him a moment. "You're difficult to figure out, Mr. Hawkins."

"And why is that?"

"I'm not sure. You just continue to surprise me."

"I promise you I am not trying to be a puzzle."

"I know." She smiled as another young girl walked up to her in adoration.

"Ms. Layla, we were wondering if you'd fly with us yet?" Her high-pitched voice in combination with her oversized brown eyes melted the woman beside him. He felt Layla completely relax as she released his arm and knelt in front of the young girl.

"I am on my way, little one." She tapped the girl's nose and the girl smiled as she turned and sprinted back towards Rose and the other girls screaming of her success in convincing Layla to play.

"It would seem I have to tend to me fairy duties, Mr. Hawkins." She walked him back towards the men. "Glad you came." She squeezed his arm and caught the curious glance of Murphy before she darted across the grass and scooped up one of the other little girls and spun her through the air. Chloe laughed along with the other girls as they stepped in line for the same treatment. Delaney's eyes stayed on Layla as she played, clearly a star amongst the girls. After spinning each child through the air, Layla crashed onto the grass and laid on her back. Immediately, several of the girls did the same. Two sat nearest her head and reached for her brown hair and began to braid as others gathered about to talk to her. Chloe eased onto her knees and began braiding flower crowns for each of the girls. Rose laid on her back next to Layla and pointed up at the clouds to decipher shapes and creatures. *Pure and innocent fun,*

Delaney thought. And it seemed Layla enjoyed every minute of it.

"She's great with the little ones," Claron interrupted and had Delaney's back snapping to attention. He hadn't realized he'd been staring for so long.

"She seems to be. Chloe as well."

"Aye. They all love them."

"What's not to love?" Murphy asked. "Beautiful women to look up to. Both successes. Kind hearts."

"Who has a kind heart?" Rhea walked up and caught the last of their conversation and slid a hand on Murphy's shoulder.

"Our sisters. And you, of course, Rhea darling." He grinned up at her and she planted a kiss on his forehead. "You charmer."

"Best be talking about me." Riley walked up with Heidi on his arm and winked at Rhea.

"Not all conversations stem around you, brother," Murphy retorted. "Sorry to disappoint." He smugly took a sip of his beer and Riley tapped the bottom of it, the beer flooding Murphy's mouth. Murphy choked and spat a bit as he beat his chest and coughed. Rhea tenderly patted him on the back as she and Heidi scolded a laughing Riley and Claron. Delaney absorbed it all. He liked watching the

O'Rifcans' interactions and he was always impressed with how they seemed to be good friends as well as siblings. He'd never quite encountered a family dynamic like theirs. He gasped in surprise at his sudden lack of oxygen as someone gripped him from behind and squeezed the bejesus out of him. A head rested in the center of his back for a brief second before he realized that what he'd just experienced was an embrace. He then felt a firm slap on his back as Mrs. O'Rifcan circled around him and squeezed Riley as well. "So glad you've come, Delaney boyo. Brightened my day, it has."

"Mammy loves new faces," Riley explained. "I think she was a wee bit nervous the family meal scared you off."

"He wouldn't be the first now, would he?" Sidna guffawed as she slipped her arm around Delaney's waist and squeezed him again, with just a tad less force. "Seems our Mr. Delaney is made of firmer stuff than the others. Glad to see it, yes I am." She looked to Claron. "Almost finished with the meats, love? I believe everyone's starting to get a mouth on them."

Claron lifted a large slab of beef and placed it on a platter Rhea held beside him. "This is the last of it, Mam."

"Ah, good. Rhea love, just take it to the picnic area when he's finished. Lorena and Aine are helping

move the rest of the food to the table now. I'll have your da call everyone to attention. If I can find him." She looked around and Claron pointed to a far stretch of land between them and Claron Senior and Roland, Rhea's grandfather. Both held fishing rods as they graced a low valley nearest the river. "That man," Sidna growled, placing her hands on her hips. "Always fishing, he is. How am I to yell all that way? He'll never hear me."

"I believe that might be the point, Mam," Murphy teased. She swatted him on the head and then lightly tugged his hair, so he had to gaze up at her. "Then I guess it is up to me young and fit son to sprint over and retrieve him, now isn't it?"

Regret and annoyance briefly crossed Murphy's face as he stood and set his beer bottle on the arm of an empty porch chair. Sighing, he pointed at Riley. "Up for a race, brother?"

Heidi looked up at Riley and grinned to see his response. He handed her his own bottle of beer and stretched his arms before him and popped the knuckles of his hands. As Murphy opened his mouth to begin the countdown, Riley took off at a sprint.

"Och, the cheat!" Murphy immediately set out after his brother as everyone laughed behind them. Riley reached the older gentlemen first but was quickly tackled to the ground as Murphy finished his sprint in a jump onto his brother's back. Arms

and legs could be seen rolling amidst the tall grass before a sharp whistle resounded from Senior's lips. The two men scrabbled apart and laughed as they reported their mother's message.

"Men." Heidi rolled her eyes as she beamed in Riley's direction.

"It's a brother's thing," Claron clarified. "We can't help it. Everything can be turned into a competition."

"Do you have brothers, Delaney?" Heidi asked.

"Ah, no. No siblings for me."

"I don't have any either," Rhea added.

"Yes, you do." Heidi pointed to all the O'Rifcans scattered about and Claron kissed Rhea's cheek as he placed the last piece of meat onto the platter.

"I guess that's true." Rhea flushed as she held up the meat. "Guess I better go put this on the table. Better find a seat somewhere," she commented to the others as she walked towards a bossy Sidna overseeing the placement of the dishes.

Heidi wandered towards the table to help settle the little girls.

"I know we can be an overwhelming bunch, but glad you came, mate." Claron reached into an ice

bucket and retrieved a fresh beer and popped the top.

"I appreciate the invite. I, ah... well, I don't quite make an effort in socializing as much as I should. On occasion. Or really ever. Well, not never..." Delaney trailed off, and attempted to erase away the awkwardness by clearing his throat, but he caught the brief, sympathetic gaze of Claron. Thankfully, the brother was too kind to keep pushing the conversation and instead motioned towards the group. "Not sure about you, Delaney, but standing over that grill and smelling the meat has made me the hungry sort. We should grab a seat before we are stuck with the fairies and unicorns." He motioned towards his niece, a happy Rose patting the seat next to her to reserve it for Claron. The man chuckled. "Well, you can escape. It would seem Rosie has other plans for me." Claron eased into the smaller chair at the lower table as Rose immediately began talking his ear off and showing him the ribbons in her hair. Delaney ventured towards Riley. At least, he figured, the brother was gifted with conversation and perhaps he could muster the nerve to last the entire meal before wishing to leave.

Another brother stepped in his path and extended his hand. "Haven't chatted with you yet, Delaney. Come, I wish for you to meet me wife, Aine. She wasn't at dinner last week due to work." He motioned for a pretty blonde woman to come

towards them. "Hello, Mr. Delaney," she said, shaking his hand. "Declan tells me you are Rhea and Heidi's boss in Limerick."

"I am, yes."

"Well, we are all so grateful to you for hiring the two of them. They've made our brothers so happy, and having them close has been a true blessing."

Not sure how to respond, Delaney simply nodded.

"Here," Aine pulled out a chair. "You have a seat here. Declan, hold a spot for me. I'm to help your mam with drinks." She kissed her husband's cheek as she walked away. The brother sat in a chair next to the one Aine had pulled out for Delaney. Delaney sat. "And what is it you do, Declan?" Delaney asked. Curious as to how such a tall man could fit his knees under the table, he contemplated Declan's dilemma until the man spoke.

"I'm a sergeant for the local Garda."

"Garda?" Surprised, Delaney leaned back in his chair. "Impressive. I didn't realize any of the O'Rifcans were in law enforcement."

"Aye. One of us has to be," Declan stated on a whisper. "You can't have seven boys in the family without there being some trouble at some point." He chuckled. "Mainly Murphy with his pub. He

sometimes abuses the privilege by calling me up when there's a squabble. But, 'tis a fine line of work for me."

"And your wife is the doctor?"

"Nurse," Declan clarified.

"Ah, that's right."

"And that's me boy there." He pointed to a young lad shadowing after another O'Rifcan brother, Jace.

"Poor kid." Delaney watched as Jace pointed for the boy to go sit with all the little girls and pure dread covered the boy's face. Declan laughed. "He's a bit used to it, but he'd rather spend time with his uncles, that's for certain."

Delaney smelled her before he saw her. The light flirtatious scent mixed with dangerously feminine undertones flooded his senses. "Dec, please don't scare away our Mr. Hawkins," Layla pleaded as she sat next to Delaney.

Conor sat across from them and beamed. "This be the boss man, is it?" He toasted his fork towards Delaney before digging into his plate full of food.

"He is," Layla replied. She watched as Chloe slid into the seat next to Conor and handed their friend a napkin before starting on her own plate of food.

"Good to see you again, Delaney," Chloe greeted. "I am sorry I have yet to say hello."

"You've been a tad busy." Delaney smiled as Chloe rolled her eyes.

"A bit. I believe I've run more today than I have the entire year." They both chuckled and Layla's eyes bounced between the two of them.

"You handled it gracefully," he complimented. He watched as a light stain of pink tainted the sister's cheeks before she continued eating. He liked Chloe. She held a sweetness about her that made him wish to know her more. Not in any romantic way. He just felt her a nice presence. And based on all he'd heard about the sister from Rhea, she seemed the likeable sort. As did the man beside her. Conor reached towards Chloe's plate and plucked one of her tomatoes. She did not object, but instead, reached towards his plate and collected a cucumber. Neither seemed to think the interaction odd or rude, they simply just continued about their business.

"Haven't you a plate, Delaney love?" Sidna walked up behind him and slid a heaping plate in front of him. "Best not go hungry today. We still have presents to be opened." She patted him on the shoulder before moving on.

"This looks wonderful," he muttered while slipping his napkin into his lap.

"I made that." Layla pointed to a mixture of veggies. "Be prepared, Mr. Hawkins, it will knock your socks off."

He smirked. "That so?" He forked a few pieces and popped them into his mouth. He paused. The flavors erupted and he slowly chewed.

"Well?" Layla asked, leaning closer to him. Her eyes sparkled as she watched him.

He nodded. "'Tis delicious, Layla. Very much so."

She winked at him as she motioned to Conor. "So, Conor, I have a mind to ask you for a wee bit of a favor."

"Oh?" The brusque man waited patiently for her to explain.

"How are you with scroll work?"

"Scroll?"

"Aye, as in legs of a stool?"

Conor rubbed a hand over his scraggly red beard a moment. "Depends. I'm not the most gifted, but I've given it a go once or twice."

"Not gifted?" Chloe asked in shock. "That be a flat lie, Conor McCarthy, and you know it. He is just being modest. Have you seen the cabinet at Roland's flat?" Chloe asked.

Layla shook her head.

"Designed him a beautiful bar piece, intricate carvings and all."

Conor blushed at the praise and Layla's brows rose in contemplation. "Then I believe I wish to hire you then, Conor. Again."

"Well, it may be a bit, I'm afraid. Ms. Chloe here has asked me to work on a couple of new display stands for her flowers, and Riley has me pretty tied up with a few custom pieces for his latest project. Not to mention Clary with his plans on a few things."

"Posh," Layla waved her hand. "You can squeeze in a couple of stools, no problem. I believe in you."

"Layla," Chloe warned.

"What?" Layla asked innocently. "I know Conor would love for me shop to look its best on opening day. Wouldn't you, Conor?"

"Of course. But that be in just a week, right?"

"Yes. Next Friday to be exact. I need two stools. I have a design in mind."

"Layla," Chloe shook her head. "One week is not near enough time. Plus, he has to work his mam's restaurant."

Delaney watched as the look of being trapped settled over Conor's features. "How about we let the man decide?" Delaney asked, hoping to give control of the conversation back to Conor.

Conor sighed, "I could try to get them done for you, Layla. I can't promise they'll be done by Friday, but I will do me best."

Layla clapped her hands together and squealed before reaching across the table and squeezing Conor's hand. "You truly are an angel, Conor McCarthy."

"And you are taking advantage of his kindness," Chloe stated openly.

"He said he could do it." Layla shrugged and then turned her attention back towards Delaney. "Now, all I have to do is convince Mr. Hawkins here to come to my grand opening, and then I will be all set." She looked to him hopefully and in pure pleasure as he knew she'd put him on the spot.

He didn't want her to think she could simply boss him into a decision, or that he would just give her what she wanted. Because it seemed Layla O'Rifcan was used to getting what she wanted. However, he found he would like to see her in action. See her work and what she was passionate about. "Well, it is on my calendar."

Layla continued her celebratory squeals as she pulled his face towards hers and kissed him soundly on the cheek. "It's going to be brilliant."

«CHAPTER EIGHT»

The final touches for the big day were coming together. Layla sat in a chair she'd stolen from Chloe's office, staring at her half of the building. Her eyes searched for anything that looked odd or for spaces that needed a little extra tending, but she found none. It was absolutely perfect. Her supplies were well stocked. The scents were pleasing, the entire aroma of the store was beautifully calm and tranquil, sweetened by vanilla. The fresh flowers in various vases that Chloe had showcased mixed well with Layla's products.

Polished, dusted, and gleaming, the shelves and stands shined, the warmth of the afternoon sun flooded the space and illuminated the vibrant

colors of her bath salts and glass bottles. A perfect mélange. She sighed and smiled happily at what she'd accomplished. Her grand opening was in two days' time. And she was ready. One hundred percent ready.

She'd sent personal invitations to all her friends. Murphy had allowed her to leave flyers on the bar and tables at his pub advertising the event. Aine had taken flyers to the hospital for her and posted them throughout. Mr. O'Malley had talked it up to every customer that'd passed through the market this week, and Rhea and Heidi posted flyers in any coffee shop or café they could visit in Limerick the last couple of weeks. She was grateful to all of them for helping her. And she hoped she had a fabulous turn out. In particular, she hoped Delaney would come. She wasn't quite sure what it was about the man that had her so intrigued, but she knew she wanted to see him again. Whether he tried to be or not, he was a puzzle to her. He didn't seem overly interested in her other than as an acquaintance. And that was odd. Or it was for Layla. She was used to snagging any man she wanted, and unfortunately some she did not. But she was a magnet for men, only apparently not to Delaney. He seemed rather fine not seeing her. She was surprised he hadn't asked for her number after Rose's party. She'd made it a point to spend as much time with him as possible. Introduced him around, sat with him, chatted with him most of the afternoon and evening. Yet at the end of the party

he walked her to her car, which was conveniently parked next to his, and simply opened her door. Nothing more. No kiss to the cheek or hand. No request for her phone number. And no request for a date. Completely odd.

She crossed her arms and rested a fist under her chin.

The bell above the door jingled and she turned to see Clary covered in dirt and grime traipsing inside.

"Stop where you are, Clary," she ordered, and pointed for him not to leave the entry rug. "I've spent me whole mornin' cleanin' the place and I am not about to have you trudging mud on me clean floors."

He grinned sheepishly. "Sorry, Layla. Been harvesting all morning. Have a small break as we wait for the additional lories to arrive for this afternoon."

"Think you will be finished by Friday?" she asked.

"Aye. If all goes well today, we should wrap up in the morning."

"Good. Because you have to come to my grand opening." She opened her arms wide to showcase her half of the store.

"It looks brilliant."

"I think so." She nodded confidently and turned in her chair, crossing her arms once more. "So, tell me what brings you by. Chloe isn't here if you be needing flowers. She's helping Conor's mam at the restaurant since Conor is busy with Riley's projects, whatever they may be."

"I don't need Chloe." Claron eased onto his rear and rested his back against the door, careful not to leave the space of the small rug. "I mean, I will eventually, but I wished to talk to you first."

"Alright, you have me ears, I'm listening." Intrigued by the sudden seriousness of Claron's face, Layla waited patiently.

"Well, it's... hmm..." He rubbed a nervous hand over his beard and then wiped the dirt on his pant leg. "I'm going to need some candles."

Her brows rose. "Alright. Candles. Not a problem. How many?"

"That's the tricky part." He looked up at her, his green eyes serious. "I'm to need the whole lot." He waved his hand around the room. "Or something close to it."

"Oh, really now? Wish to buy me out before I even open me doors, do you? And what, dear Clary, do you plan to do with all me candles?"

Claron ran a hand over the back of his neck before looking up at his sister again. "Well, I aim to ask Rhea to marry me."

His words hung in the air a minor second before Layla jumped to her feet and squealed. She ran over to him and dropped to her knees to hug him as he sat. He laughed. "I haven't done it yet, Layla."

"I know, but we've all been waiting for this day. When? When do you wish to ask her, Clary?"

He shrugged. "When I'm ready. When I have everything ready."

"And what all is there to have ready?"

"Well, first, I need to ask her father for his blessing."

"Which he will give," Layla added. "As well as Roland."

"Aye. I've already discussed the matter with Roland."

"One step done." Layla mimicked a check mark in the air. "What else? What's your plan?"

"That's where I need help."

"Seems everyone needs me help in planning these days." Layla grinned.

"You're one of the best at it," Claron explained, his compliment warming her.

"Alright, so tell me what you have planned so far."

"You can't laugh."

Layla giggled. "And why would I laugh?"

"Because I'm no good at this, and I want it to be perfect. Yet, I don't know if it is a good idea, or if it's just me thinkin' it will be. I may be completely out of my head. God knows I've been half out of me mind since Roland gave me the ring."

"Roland gave you a ring?"

"Aye. Family heirloom, if I wish to use it."

Layla held a hand to her heart. "That be sweet and royally kind of our dear Roland."

"Aye. Agreed."

Layla clapped her hands. "Tell me your plan and I will do my best in helping it come together."

Nervously, Claron began pouring out his wishes and Layla hopped to her feet to grab a notebook and began jotting down notes. He had a plan. A great one. One that would mean the world to Rhea, and Layla loved that Clary had found a woman so worthy of it all. Layla looked around her shop at what candle stock she had. It would take

her a couple of weeks to make enough candles for his big night, but no matter how knackered she felt already, she would see to it that his order was completed as soon as possible.

She reached over and squeezed his hand. "I love you, Clary, and I think we know Rhea will say yes no matter how you propose, but I'm completely in awe of your plan to make it special for her."

"Isn't it supposed to be?"

"Aye, 'tis. But not all choose such grand plans."

"I wish to hold nothing back when it comes to Rhea. I'd give her the world if I could."

"And we all know it. So does she. I imagine that is part of your charm." Layla winked at him as she stood to her feet and reached a hand down to help him to his own. "Consider this order officially placed. I will also help in the grand plan." She wriggled her eyebrows. "I'll partner with Chloe and we'll work out the logistics. You handle the brothers."

"Aye. I be telling Riley tonight. I hope he will keep his mouth shut and not let it slip. Though I know Rhea knows I wish to spend me life with her, I would still like to surprise her with this."

"'Tis important enough, Riley will keep his trap closed. We will just threaten certain death if he does not."

Laughing, Claron nodded. "That we will. Thank you, Layla, for helping your lowly brother woo his lass."

"Oh, anytime now. Anytime." She winked as he opened the door and walked out. Heaving a happy sigh, she patted the notebook against her palm and walked over to her work counter. She then began to draft a list of supplies. She would definitely need to make a trip to Limerick to stock up on what she'd need. And as that thought occurred to her, she thought she might just need to make a pitstop at Rhea's work in the process, only not to talk to Rhea, but to Delaney. For if there was to be an engagement party, she would need to make sure he marked it on his calendar.

∞

Delaney held up a finger as his secretary lingered in his doorway and he continued to listen to the caller on the other end of the phone. He'd asked his secretary to interrupt him if she saw his call took longer than a half hour. What he didn't expect was for her to have a real reason to. Apparently, he had a visitor.

"Quite so," he spoke into the phone. "I will see to it. No concerns on our end." He paused. "And thank

you. Yes... have a care." He placed the phone in its cradle and looked up. "Yes?"

"A visitor for you, Mr. Hawkins." She stepped out of the way and Layla O'Rifcan strutted inside. She smiled sweetly at the secretary.

"Thank you, Lena." The secretary smiled and nodded farewell to her boss before quietly closing his door.

Layla looked him over and Delaney felt the slightest urge to fidget under her bold stare, but he silently waited for her to speak.

"Are you not surprised to see me?" she asked.

He tilted his head and linked his hands on his desk. "Yes, I suppose I am. What brings you by my office, Layla? Here to see Rhea?"

"No. Actually I'm hoping she doesn't see me while I'm here. Bold move coming during work hours, I know, but I didn't have any other way of contacting you."

His brow rose and she continued.

"I need to speak with you about an important matter involving our Rhea."

He leaned forward, concern evident as he spoke. "Is she not well?"

Confused, Layla leaned back in her chair. "Of course she is, why wouldn't she be?"

"Oh," He leaned back in his own chair. "Your tone just seemed to suggest it was something serious. I just assumed."

Layla waved her hand to erase their departure from the real topic. "No, no, no, no... this has nothing to do about Rhea's health, it's about her and Clary."

"I see." He didn't see. He still wasn't quite sure why Layla felt he needed to know anything about Rhea and Claron.

His cell phone rang, and he was quite relieved, afraid the current conversation would take a turn he didn't wish to hear. He held up his hand to Layla to stop further conversation a moment as he answered.

"Ah, Chloe. Thank you for returning my call. So sorry to bother you."

"Chloe?" Layla asked. "My sister?"

He nodded as his hand covered the receiver at her outburst. He then went back to the phone. "So you listened to my message?" A pause. "Perfect. Yes, I was hoping you would say yes. Today?" He glanced at his watch. "I could probably sneak away a few minutes early and meet you

there. That would be great, Chloe. I look forward to it." He hung up and then looked at Layla. Her cheeks reddened, and he saw a storm brewing in her eyes.

"Why is me sister calling you at work?"

"I'm to meet with her later."

"Oh, are you now?" she bit out as she crossed her arms.

"Yes."

His obliviousness to her temper simply fueled her further.

"I see. Well, excuse me for bothering you, Mr. Hawkins." She stood, straightening her blouse before she stomped towards the door. "I can see you're very busy and it would seem you have other things on your mind."

"Layla," His voice stopped her from turning the knob of the door and she turned. "You came to tell me something." He motioned to the chair she'd just vacated. "No need to storm off because of interruptions. I assure you there will be no others."

She crossed her arms, dissatisfaction evident in her stiff posture and tight jaw.

"Have I offended you in some way?" He asked, curious as to why she turned so cold.

She uncrossed her arms and stalked back to the vacant chair and sat on a huff. "No. And yes," she replied honestly. "But it doesn't matter." She mustered her dignity and continued. "Clary wishes to ask Rhea to marry him and we need you in on the plot for the big day."

"I see. Now that is something indeed." He steepled his fingers on his desk. "When does he plan to ask her?"

"Not sure yet. He's trying to line everyone up. He has a beautiful plan. Your part will be to make sure Rhea leaves work on time that Friday and heads to Castlebrook. No keeping her late."

"I believe I can do that. Seems like a simple enough role."

Layla sighed. "Yes, we hope so. But you know our Rhea. A work horse, she is. No giving her a new project before closing time or she will stay to work a bit more."

"You have my word."

"Good. I will let Clary know. He is still finetuning the details. He just asked me to run it by you while I was in town today shopping for supplies."

"I will do whatever I need to help."

"Good. I'll make sure he knows it." She stood. "I must go. I have supplies to buy and the messages for the shop. Chloe bought everything except the tea. And that's a must have."

"If she's needing tea, I can always take it to her when I meet with her later. I don't mind."

"I'm sure you don't," Layla grumbled.

Again, Delaney eyed her curiously.

"'Tis fine. The tea is for me to have at the shop, not Chloe. She's a coffee drinker. But you two enjoy your little rendezvous. I'm sure 'twill be a blast." Layla flicked her hair over her shoulder as she made her way towards the door.

"Rendezvous?" Delaney chuckled. "Are you aggravated with me? For visiting your sister?"

Layla's cheeks flushed. "Absolutely not."

"Are you sure? You seem… offended that I would be spending time with Chloe."

"Just surprised is all. You only spoke to her minimally at the party on Saturday and now you be taking off early from your work to see her. Just seems a bit odd." Layla shrugged.

Delaney bit back a grin. Layla was jealous of Chloe. Clearly Layla wished for him to want to visit her instead of her sister. *Interesting*, he thought.

He couldn't remember the last time a woman wished to spend time with him. He cringed at that thought. Not that he wished for a woman to spend time with, just that he worked too much to include one in his daily life. He shook his head. The last thing he needed was to rationalize his own choices in front of company. "Well, I plan to stop to visit Murphy afterwards at the pub. If you're back in Castlebrook by then, you should stop by for a pint."

"And listen to the two of you banter back and forth? I think not." She peeked out the door to make sure Rhea was not anywhere near the office door. Delaney stood and began walking her direction. She shut the door. "What are you doing?"

"I was planning on walking you to the elevator. Like a gentleman." He smirked.

"No. I don't want to draw attention to me presence. If Rhea sees me, she'll be suspicious."

"Rhea is working, Layla. She won't be exiting her office for quite some time. I assure you." He reached for the knob and turned it. "After you."

Layla quietly walked down the hall and peeked around the corner before entering the lobby. She hastened her steps towards the elevator and Delaney chuckled behind her. She pressed the button and sighed in relief. "I hate being sneaky

around her. Feels so dishonest. But 'tis for her own good. The surprise will be worth it."

"Sounds like an exciting plan is in the works. I can't wait to hear the rest of it." Delaney could hear the phone ring and the secretary answer. He heard her mention his name and waved for the secretary to take a message. She acknowledged him with a nod and her eyes went back to her pen and pad.

"I can wait here on me own. You have calls, Mr. Hawkins. Best not let the day slip away."

"Are you trying to be rid of me?"

"Aye, because you've work to do." Layla's eyes widened as she stepped closer to him so as to hide behind his slim frame. She ducked her head to be level with his chest and he heard her mumble an unladylike phrase as Rhea called out her name.

"Layla, is that you? What are you doing here?" Rhea's heels clacked along the floor as she started towards them.

Layla looked up at Delaney for help and he just shrugged his shoulders. She quickly straightened and leaned into him. "Your help starts now, Mr. Hawkins," she whispered, her hand sliding around the back of his neck and pulling his lips to hers.

Shock fired through him at the contact. And though the kiss was chaste and a bit forceful, his arms were full of Layla as she leaned further into him so as to sell their impromptu kiss as something more. When she pulled away, she turned to a shocked Rhea. "Just visiting Mr. Hawkins here." Layla flirtatiously winked at Delaney and straightened his tie as she turned her attention to Rhea. "Sorry I didn't come say hi. I was a bit... busy." She mustered a small giggle that gave Rhea the completely wrong impression. Rhea looked to Delaney and a slow smile spread over her face.

"Wow. I didn't realize you guys had hit it off so well." She playfully punched Delaney's shoulder as she stepped towards the secretary's desk. "I'll let you two go about your day. I was just running these over to scan. See you later, Layla."

Layla wriggled her fingers in farewell and as soon as Rhea's back turned the elevator doors swooshed open. She stepped inside and turned to face Delaney. "You aren't riding down with me?"

"No."

She laughed at his confused expression. "Pity."

"I... we... she has to know that was not real," he stated.

Layla lunged towards him and grabbed his elbow, the elevator doors bouncing off her purse as they attempted to close. "No, she does not. We cannot have her questioning my presence here today. It was one small kiss to divert her thinking. Completely harmless. Do *not* tell her it was false, Delaney, or I will have your head." She pointed at his face and then lightly nudged his glasses up his nose for him. He took a cautious step back.

"Very well. I will not say anything about it. And if she asks, I'll just..."

"Lie. You will lie, Delaney. 'Tis alright to say the dirty word." Layla laughed as she stepped back into the elevator.

"I will not lie. I will just say it was a surprise."

Layla rolled her eyes. "Very well then. Perhaps I'll *surprise* you again later in Castlebrook. Though if Rhea catches you kissing Chloe as well, then we may have a problem with our story."

"Why on Earth would I kiss your sister?" His voice rose as he took offense and she tilted her head to study him.

"Why wouldn't you? If things go well this evening, 'tis a typical response after a lovely night."

"What are you talking about?" He held his hands out in question. "I'm meeting her to order flowers for my assistants for appreciation day next week."

Layla's mouth fell open as her cheeks turned scarlet.

Delaney just shook his head, a tired smile crossing his face. "You know what? I think this is a good moment for me to walk back to my office. Have a care, Layla." He was completely baffled. Layla thought him interested in Chloe and yet here she stood giving him a kiss so as to thwart suspicion from Rhea about Claron's plans. He shook his head. Too much. There was too much happening in such a short amount of time. He'd just met the O'Rifcans, and already they were giving him a headache. Rhea owed him for all this. Big time.

«CHAPTER NINE»

"*I'm telling you, Clary*, the plan is genius. Rhea will melt into a puddle at your feet once she reaches the cottage." Layla watched as her brother nervously ran his hand through his hair—again—as he pored over his plans of proposal.

"I agree, brother," Riley chimed in. "A proper proposal plan." He grinned at his own alliteration. "And you needn't worry, Layla has Delaney lined up to make sure Rhea leaves on time. I will intercept her at O'Brien's Bridge and will report to Layla when I do. You will know where Rhea is at all times before her reaching the cottage."

"Yes. Good. I just... 'tis a bit nerve racking is all."

Riley slapped him on the back. "It should be. Just the rest of your life you're plannin' and all."

"Gee, thank you, brother. I feel so at ease." Claron rolled his eyes as Layla grinned.

"Nothing to worry about Clary. She loves you. You and Rhea share a love others can only wish for."

"Speak for yourself," Riley mumbled, thinking of his Heidi.

"Well, most people wish for." Layla shook her head at Riley's interruption. "Everything will go according to plan and you will make lovely Rhea your beautiful bride."

Claron leaned back in his chair and sighed happily. "Crazy thought, but I like the sound of it."

"Aye, me too." Layla squeezed his hand. "Now put these away." She waved her hand over the architectural drafts Riley had brought over for Claron to look at. "Don't want them catching a spill."

"I have copies," Riley assured Claron.

Claron rolled up the papers and slipped them into a protective tube. "I think I will shower and then head to the pub. Harvesting is officially done. I'm exhausted, and I will not be seeing Rhea until tomorrow, so I wish to share company with me friends."

"As if you couldn't if she were here," Layla replied with offense on Rhea's behalf.

"Oh, no." Claron stood. "I didn't mean that I couldn't do that with Rhea here. I just meant... well, she is not here for me to share company with and I'm in the mood to be social."

"For once," Riley teased.

"Aye, so I might as well enjoy a pint."

"Mam will be upset you're skipping the meal," Layla warned.

"She has plenty of guests this week to cluck over. One less mouth to feed should be a blessing," Claron stated.

"Make that two mouths. I'm venturing to the pub as well." Riley stood and slipped his keys from his pocket. "Wish to carpool, brother?"

"Aye. After me shower."

"Ah, yes. There is that." Riley wrinkled his nose. "I'll wait. And what of you, sister? Coming to the pub?"

"Of course I am. 'Tis the night before my big grand opening. I need to make sure everyone there plans to attend."

Riley laughed. "Always the business woman these days, our Layla." He lightly tugged on her hair as she pointed for Claron to walk down the hall and go take care of his business.

"As I should be. Layla's Potions is me livelihood now. Especially once you and Clary tear the cottage to pieces. I can't rent it out to a bunch of Yanks if it is a pile of rubble."

"You always have the café," Riley pointed out.

"Aye, I will admit Mam's been rather patient with me. Flexible and what not. I can't remember the last time I've put a full day in of waiting tables."

"Preparation is key. Even Mam knows that." Riley added. "She wants you to succeed so she will make allowances."

Layla worried her bottom lip. "Can I ask you something, brother?"

Riley crossed his arms and leaned against the kitchen counter. "Ask away."

"Do you think me mad for doing this?"

"What? Opening your shop? Not a'tall. 'Tis a brilliant idea. And you're gifted, there's no denying that."

"It's just, I worry about... well, lots of things. But I worry people will not want to buy from me."

"And why wouldn't they?"

Layla narrowed her eyes and tilted her head as if he should know the answer to his question.

"Ah, worried about the reputation, are you?"

"Yes. Though I wasn't until just the other day. I don't regret a thing I've done, just concerned that some of those things might prevent some locals from venturing into me shop."

Riley threw his head back and laughed. "Steal too many lads, have you, sister? Afraid the women won't want to buy from such a homewrecker?" He bellowed as she swatted him.

"I've never been a homewrecker, Riley O'Rifcan, and you best watch your tongue."

"Ah, but you have been a heartbreaker, and that's what has you concerned," he pointed out.

"Somewhat."

"I say, forget about it. You have plenty of willing customers, and you will have new ones. Who needs the naysayers?"

"I do. I need any customer I can fetch."

"Not true. Just you wait and see, Layla. Your brews are about to be a staple in Castlebrook and the rest of County Clare. Just you wait."

A small smile titled her lips as she reluctantly walked into his open embrace for a quick hug of encouragement. It ended with him squeezing her so tightly, her feet lifted off the floor. When he set her right again, Claron entered the room.

"Thanks for waiting."

"Don't mention it, brother." Riley waved for them to follow him outside. "Come now, its our night to treat our sister to a pint. For tomorrow she will be a grand success."

Smiling to herself, Layla thanked the heavens for her brothers. All of them. She also threw in a few requests for a successful grand opening. Her siblings would not let her down. If she had zero customers tomorrow, she could at least count on her siblings to show up and make her night a grand one regardless. And that, she thought, was worth more than any riches. However, while she prayed for miracles, she also mentioned Delaney. Perhaps he would indeed show up and help make her night a bit brighter.

∞

Music. Laughter. Chatter. Delaney wasn't in the mood. But Rhea and Heidi both clenched their hands together and pleaded.

"Come, Delaney, please." Rhea smirked. "You have absolutely no plans and we are asking you to come spend the evening with friends."

"Friends, are we?" he asked.

Heidi frowned and then propped her hands on her hips. "Don't be pompous, you know you like us."

Delaney chuckled and the women grinned. "Fine," he sighed. "I'll make an appearance. But I have currently spent the last two weekends in Castlebrook. This will be the third in a row. After tonight, I have met my quota."

"You mean after tomorrow," Heidi corrected.

"Why tomorrow?" Delaney asked.

"Layla's grand opening," Rhea reminded him with a stern scowl.

"Ah, yes. The opening." He sighed again and leaned back in his office chair staring up at them.

"Delaney..." Rhea warned.

"I will be there, Rhea."

"Good. Layla needs as much support as possible."

Delaney stood and buttoned his suit jacket.

"Where are you going?" Heidi asked, as he walked towards his door.

"I'm leaving. Aren't we to go have drinks?" His mouth tipped into a sly smirk as the women hurried after him towards the lobby.

"I have to grab my purse," Rhea called, her heels hurriedly making their way down the hall towards her office.

"Grab mine on your way!" Heidi called, pressing the elevator button. She smiled at Delaney. "I'm glad you're coming."

He tilted his head. "Why is that?"

Heidi stepped closer to him and whispered. "Rhea told me she saw you and Layla kissing." She punched him slightly in the shoulder. "Didn't know you were such a romantic, Del."

He groaned at the nickname and she laughed as she winked. "I couldn't help it."

"Well, it wasn't a real kiss," he explained. Heidi's brows rose. "Layla was here to talk to me of Claron's proposal and Rhea walked up and spotted her. Layla felt it would deter any questions if it seemed like she was here visiting me for... other reasons."

Heidi burst into laughter and just shook her head. "That sly little fox."

"Indeed."

Heidi crossed her arms and leaned against the wall. "So how was the kiss?"

His eyes widened at her audacity and she just laughed harder as Rhea walked up and handed over her purse.

"Okay, let's go. Layla would never forgive us if we are late." They stepped into the vacant elevator.

"We'll more than likely arrive early." Heidi reached into her purse and grabbed a slice of gum and popped it into her mouth. She offered the pack towards Rhea and Delaney and both shook their heads. "Riley was in Galway today, I imagine he won't be there until closer to seven."

"Murphy will be there and Chloe, I'm sure." Rhea scrolled through her cell phone and smiled.

"Oh Lord, she's received a message from Claron." Heidi playfully rolled her eyes as Rhea shoved her friend's shoulder.

Delaney watched the numbers tick by as they made their way smoothly to the bottom floor and the parking lot. "I will be along shortly." He unlocked his car.

"Where are you going?" Rhea asked, pausing by her own door, Heidi already standing halfway inside the passenger side.

"Are you two always this nosy?"

Rhea flushed as Heidi nodded unashamedly.

Delaney just shook his head. "I'm grabbing a coffee."

"Oh. Okay." Relief washed over Rhea's features.

"It's been a long week, and if I'm to be social for the evening I need a bit of caffeine to boost my energy. I will be along."

"You better." Heidi narrowed her gaze and held two fingers in front of her eyes before then turning them to point at Delaney.

He saluted on a laugh as he slipped into his car and set out to the nearest drive-thru coffee house.

∞

Layla paused at the doorway to Murphy's Pub as she spotted Rhea and Heidi pulling into the parking lot. She waved in greeting as the two women hurried towards her with excited, open arms.

"You look beautiful," Rhea complimented, spinning Layla into a circle. "That dress is gorgeous."

Layla ran a hand down the slimming plum dress. The hem line graced mid-thigh and the plunging neckline had her grateful for double-sided tape, but overall, her choice of wardrobe confirmed what she planned to do. And that was to

draw attention. Drum up excitement for her grand opening tomorrow, and if that required a bit of flirting and sultry glances, she'd do it.

Heidi opened the door and the room fell quiet. Murphy beamed as he hopped on top of his bar and motioned towards the door. "And here be my sister now! The amazing Layla of Layla's Potions!" Layla entered to cheers and toasts. She blew Murphy a kiss as she accepted hugs on her way into the building. She reached the bar and looked to a man seated on a stool, her ex, Gage O'Donaghue. She extended her hand and he helped her step her way onto the bar top as well. Murphy gripped her hand as he continued to proclaim:

"For every wound, a balm.

For every sorrow, cheer.

For every storm, a calm.

For every thirst, a beer!"

Cheers erupted as everyone chugged back a sip of their choice of drink.

"Discounted drinks all the night long in honor of my dear sister! Except those who drink to forget, you will please pay in advance!"

Laughter sounded throughout the room as everyone clapped. Layla bowed and waved as Murphy handed her a pint.

"To Layla!" Sentiments echoed as again another toast rose throughout the room. She lightly kissed Murphy's cheek as Gage helped her down from the bar. She patted him on the shoulder in thanks as she made her way towards Heidi and Rhea.

"Now that is a sweet endorsement." Rhea hugged her as she waved to Declan across the room.

"Aye. Murphy be grand."

"Chloe should be here in a moment." As if she knew her name had been spoken, the youngest O'Rifcan sibling walked in followed by Conor. Conor caught Layla's eye and trudged his way towards her with heavy steps and sparkling eyes. He grabbed her hand and spun her out and back into his arms and dipped her towards the floor before popping her back to her feet.

"Celebrating successes has me in the mood for dancing, lass. Best be prepared." He guffawed as he released her and made his way to the bar.

"That man." Layla just shook her head as Heidi and Rhea laughed.

Chloe ventured closer to their conversation and squeezed Layla's hand in sisterly support. "Good turn out so far, sister," she whispered.

"Aye, though most seem to be ignoring me." Layla sighed.

"The Irish ignore anything they can't drink or punch," Chloe commented.

"Aye, 'tis true." Layla relaxed on a laugh.

"What's that about punching?" Claron walked up and hugged his sister before swooping Rhea in for a kiss. "I found a straggler on me way in." He pointed over Layla's shoulder and she turned to find Delaney standing at the bar accepting his first pint from Murphy. The two men shook hands and Delaney laughed at whatever comment Murphy tossed his way. He appeared relaxed, his usual stiff button-up was rolled at the sleeves. He'd ditched his tie and let loose the button at the top of his shirt. Though he still looked the part of businessman, Layla could not help but see a friendliness about him that hadn't been there the last time she saw him. He walked up and clinked his glass with Heidi's.

"Good of you to show up," she murmured, and Delaney quirked a brow over the top of his glass as he took a sip. He then turned towards Layla.

"Good to see you, Layla. An early congratulations for tomorrow evening." He nodded.

"Mr. Hawkins." Layla tried to appear nonchalant, but she was shocked to see him. Yes, he'd said he might show up to her opening, but tonight? She winked at him as she stepped closer to him. She saw him swallow as his Adam's apple bobbed

slowly at her closeness. "You'll save me a dance, won't you?"

"I don't dance." He took another sip of his drink.

"We'll see about that." Layla set her glass on a nearby table. "For now, I think I will find someone who does. 'Tis a night for celebrating and all. Conor! Take me for a spin."

The boisterous redhead set his beer down and immediately obliged. Rhea laughed as his steps faltered at the beginning of the dance. Chloe just rolled her eyes in amusement as Delaney watched. "He's really quite terrible, isn't he?"

All the women laughed and nodded.

"But he's the most fun," Heidi added.

"That he is," Rhea concurred as she snuggled closer to Claron.

"I'd like to think I'm the most fun, but the heart wants what the heart wants," Claron replied and accepted the jab from Rhea's elbow as she shook her head in mock dismay.

Conor walked up in a pant as he accepted the half-finished beer from Claron and washed it down. "Already been passed over. The downfall of dancing with Layla O'Rifcan." He laughed heartily as he spotted Gage watching Layla on the dance floor. "He still a bit sour?" he asked quietly as all

turned to see the studious stance Gage had taken on.

"I don't believe so," Chloe said. "Though I guess it could be hard to see your ex moving on if you don't feel the same progression in your own life."

"He stuck?" Conor asked.

Chloe shrugged. "Just heard his latest work deal fell through. Perhaps that's the reason for his brooding."

"That or the front of Layla's dress," Claron muttered and accepted another jab to the ribs. "What?" He looked to Rhea. "I'm her brother, I'm supposed to make comments like that."

"Speaking of brothers, where be Riley?" Chloe asked.

"Galway." Heidi looked at her phone. "He should be arriving soon. I hope."

"Don't be sad, dear Heidi." Claron winked. "Riley and I rode together. He's just outside making his calls." Heidi immediately brightened.

"I'm pleased you made it, Delaney." Chloe motioned towards his empty glass. "Another?" She nodded for him to follow her to the bar.

Layla circled around the dance floor from partner to partner and spotted Delaney and Chloe

taking seats at the bar. Her sister spoke openly with him and Delaney seemed at ease in her presence. Yes, she knew they had met for flower orders, but he dedicated more time to talking with Chloe than he did to her. In fact, she'd watched him the last half hour and he hadn't glanced at her once. *Not once.* She'd all but spun in front of him whilst dancing with Jace's friend, Patrick. But nothing. Not even a nod. The song ended, and as the next began to play, Layla took a step back and thanked her partner. She needed a breather, and she also needed to break up the chat fest between Delaney and her sister. It was her special night, not Chloe's, and Delaney was hers. *Hers?* Her *what?* She shook that thought away. It didn't matter what he was to her, all that mattered was that he *was* hers. Simple. Her customer. Her friend. Her challenge. Hers. Chloe knew better than to interfere.

Layla slid a hand over Delaney's shoulders as she walked up and he jolted in his seat at the touch. He relaxed a small fraction when he saw it was her, but not much. "You have a role to play, Mr. Hawkins, don't you remember?" She nodded in Rhea's direction, their friend enraptured in a conversation with Claron and several other friends.

"It doesn't appear she notices anything afoot."

"What would be?" Chloe asked.

Layla then told of her encounter at Rhea's office and the younger sister gaped. "Layla!" She shook her head. "You cannot force Delaney into such situations. 'Tis unfair."

Layla shrugged. "It worked, did it not?" She started to sit on Delaney's leg and he shifted so as to scoot far enough over she could sit on the stool instead. Her lips twitched at his sudden awkwardness. She draped her arm around his shoulder. "I'm so glad you are here. Means the world to me, having such a loyal customer come all this way."

Delaney looked heavenward and Layla laughed. "I'm determined, Mr. Hawkins."

"It would seem. I cannot fault you for persistence."

"Aye, I can be quite persistent." Layla lowered her voice and leaned closer to him her eyes flashing to his lips before she met his gaze.

"Stop scaring the lad, Layla, and go have your fun with someone else." Murphy swiped his towel over the counter just opposite them and he grinned at the gratitude he saw in Delaney's desperate gaze towards him.

"Don't be rude, brother. I was just having a chat with my dear, Mr. Hawkins. Thanking him and all."

"Ah, is that what you were doing?" He motioned to her draped arm and seductive pose as she still leaned into Delaney. Layla scowled. "Yes. However, being the guest of honor, I suppose I should make the rounds once again. Need to rope them in for tomorrows grand event." She winked.

"Probably not the best business plan, sister." Murphy pointed to her flirtatious stance once again and Layla hopped to her feet. "And what would you know, Murphy?"

Murphy's shoulders rose a brief second. "I don't know... perhaps the fact you're sitting in me very establishment—my *successful* establishment—means I might know a thing or two." His jaw stiffened, and Chloe waved a napkin between the two.

"Stop it the both of ye," she warned. "'Tis supposed to be a night of celebration for Layla. Up to her how she spends it, brother."

Pleased, Layla winked at her sister. "And off I go to do just that."

They watched her swagger off and Murphy whistled. "You've got your hands full there, Delaney."

Delaney choked on his beer. "Pardon?"

Murphy pointed to his rambunctious sister.

"Why would my hands have anything to do with Layla?"

Murphy quirked his head. "Hmm… would you look at that, sister? I believe we've found a man immune to Layla's charms." Murphy leaned forward and pinched Delaney's arm. "He's real."

Chloe swatted her brother as he laughed. "Pay him no mind, Delaney. Murphy seems to forget that in order for his pub to continue thriving he must move along and *work*." She waved her brother away.

"Pay no mind to Layla either. 'Tis her way to flaunt about."

"It would seem so."

Chloe eyed him curiously as Delaney watched her sister across the room with a disapproving glower. Layla laughed and lightly ran a hand over another man's arm. Sighing in disappointment, Chloe stood. She extended a hand towards Delaney. "Come, Delaney. No brooding is allowed on a Friday night. Friday's are for fun and friends." She pulled him towards the rest of her family and Riley, who had finally appeared from chatting on his phone outside.

"Del?" Riley's smile widened. "I say, we just can't seem to scare you enough, can we?" He shook

Delaney's hand and laughed as Heidi shot him a look of warning.

"Good to see you, Riley. Galway coming along?"

"Slowly but surely." Beaming, Riley switched positions with Heidi so as to carry on conversation with Delaney and to thwart off the daggers he sensed from his sister across the room.

Layla growled under her breath as she continued shooting glances Delaney's way. The man still had shown no interest in spending time with her. Perplexed, Layla walked towards the bar for a fresh drink. She needed to reevaluate.

«CHAPTER TEN»

Delaney felt his feet dragging as he walked towards his car. Claron nodded for him to hold up and jogged over. "Best be making your way to the B&B, lad. Rhea's already called the mammy to ensure you have a room."

"That's kind, but I didn't pack any clothes for tomorrow."

"Sure, you did." He pointed up the street towards several boutiques and then grinned. "Mammy's expecting you. On with ye."

Delaney hesitated a moment.

"Trust me, Delaney, 'tis not a bother or an intrusion. Mam loves to have someone to cluck

over." He slapped Delaney on the shoulder as he headed towards his own truck. Rhea awaited him, and Delaney watched as they hugged and said their goodnights. Riley exited the pub with Heidi clinging piggy-back style to him. He set her down by Rhea's car and kissed her. "Keep an eye on our ladies, Del?" he asked, as he turned to walk towards Claron's truck. Heidi and Rhea backed out of the parking lot and headed towards the B&B. He eyed Murphy's Pub a moment longer, the music still drifting through every beam of wood that comprised the rustic framework. The door opened, and Layla stepped out, her arm linked with a man he recognized from earlier in the evening as her ex-boyfriend. She paused when she spotted him. Kissing the man's cheek in farewell, she walked over to him. "Fancy meeting you outside."

"Just leaving."

"You be off to limerick then, Mr. Hawkins?"

Shaking his head, he pointed in the direction of Sidna's B&B. "Your mother is kind enough to offer me a room."

"That's three weekends in a row you've spent in Castlebrook. Are we growing on you?"

"Just keeping my appointments." He smirked as her musical laughter drifted in the breeze.

"Care to give me a ride to my flat?"

"Did he not offer?" Delaney pointed to Gage sliding into his vehicle across the parking lot.

"Aye, he did. But I'd rather ride with you."

Unsure why, Delaney nodded and walked around the vehicle to open his passenger door. Layla grinned as she ducked inside.

As he climbed behind the wheel, she reached over to turn his music on. Strings of Mozart filtered through the car. Layla shook her head. "Of all things to be on a man's stereo on a Friday night, classical should not be one of them"

"And why is that?"

'Tis a night for fun, not... whatever that is."

"Then I guess a silent car ride it is then." *Easy enough*, Delaney thought.

"Silent? Are we not to talk on the way home?"

"I suppose we can. What is there to talk about?"

She crossed her arms and leaned back into the cushions and thought. "Well, for starters you will need to be heading that way to head towards my house." She pointed, and he turned obediently. "I live close to Roland."

As if he knew where Rhea's grandfather lived, Delaney mused. But he kept silent.

"Aren't you going to ask me how my night was?"

He cast her a quick look and she stared at him expectantly.

"Alright," he replied. "How was your night, Layla?"

"Darling," she added "Layla darling. It's my family's way to tack on an extra endearment." She waved for him to try again.

"Okay, Layla darling, how was your night?"

She leaned her head back against the headrest and closed her eyes as a soft smile curved her lips as he spoke. "Sounds much sweeter when you say it." She opened one eye and peeked at him as he navigated the streets. She pointed to which complex was hers. "My night was wondrous, Delaney dear, wondrous."

His left brow rose above his glasses. "You called me Delaney."

"Aye, 'tis your name isn't it?"

"Yes, but you never call me by it. Always Mr. Hawkins."

"Yes, well, tonight I wish to call you Delaney."

He pulled into a vacant spot and parked the car.

"Roland, bless him, leaves his light on so as to brighten my sidewalk. Come."

She unbuckled and hopped out of his car and waited in front of it as he inwardly tried to decipher her invitation. He wasn't the type of man who fancied a casual dalliance on a Friday night. Though he wasn't much for relationships, he still appreciated the idea of one and not a random fling. And he was still trying to figure out what kind of woman Layla O'Rifcan was. Though he remembered her tearful conversation with Rhea at the office about her reputation, the Layla he saw working the room tonight contradicted the idea of a woman with hurt feelings. He met her at the hood of his car.

Pleased, Layla linked her arm in his and walked up the small staircase and unlocked the door boasting a tarnished gold twenty-three. She flicked a lamp on as she walked inside and placed her keys on a hook by the door. Delaney stood across the threshold.

"Care to come in?" she asked

"No, thank you. I'm already indebted to your mother for putting me up for the night. I hate to abuse her kindness by being even later than I am now."

"Mam is used to late night guests. Especially with Heidi in the house. Most of the time she is coming in from Galway some weekends. Mammy won't mind."

"That may be, but I'm quite tired, so I will just be leaving."

Delaney surveyed Layla's interior. Her flat was decorated in bold colors, heavy fabrics, and luxe textures. What furniture she had looked to be secondhand, though she covered the pieces in mismatched blankets or slip covers. Ornate pillows decorated with tassels, sequins, catchy phrases, or knit detail crowded every vacant seat. Delaney felt the odd sensation of stepping into a tent at a circus, Madam Layla standing to the side as she waited to tell him his fortune.

The space was small. Just enough room to maneuver around all her furniture pieces that she seemed to have expertly placed in a unique puzzle so as not to look too overcrowded. "I will see you tomorrow." His eyes finally bounced back to hers.

She stepped towards him and slipped her arms around his waist. He stiffened as she hugged him. He felt her lightly chuckle. "You need to loosen up, Delaney. 'Tis just a friendly hug farewell. And a kiss." She rose on her tiptoes and kissed his cheek before releasing him and stepping away. "I'm pleased you came tonight. 'Twas a nice surprise. I was hoping to spend more time with you, perhaps dance, but it seemed you had other interests this evening."

Confused, Delaney tilted his head "I was just talking to those I knew. And I told you I do not dance."

"Meh" she shrugged as if his reason meant nothing. "A shame. For I'm a good dancer."

"I could tell. You danced with many a man tonight."

She bit back a smile at his haughty attitude before taking a large step towards him again. "Did that bother you?" Her voice hovered between provocative and annoyed.

"No." Which was the truth. Though he did admit to himself, he thought Layla would mingle around him a bit more. But he was able to study her instead. Her attitude and relationship amongst friends. He liked studying people. Their actions typically did speak louder than words, and Layla O'Rifcan's actions shouted with every move she made.

"I see." She fingered the button he'd loosened at the beginning of the night. "I guess it is a good thing I don't have feelings for you then, otherwise I might be offended."

"Indeed. Have a good night, Layla."

He attempted to walk away, and she grabbed his hand and pulled him back towards her. Her eyes searched his before she pressed her

lips to his. The shock of the moment had him frozen in place for a moment. When he realized he'd lost the upper hand on the evening, he simply pushed her away. She stepped towards him again and he held up his hand. "I bid you goodnight, Layla." Turning, he hurried down the steps to his car and drove away. He could see her standing in the doorway until he turned out of sight.

He knew he had probably offended her at his abrupt departure, but he wasn't about to keep kissing a woman he knew nothing about. Yes, she was friends with Rhea and Heidi. She had a lovely family. She seemed driven in her business pursuits... perhaps driven in general. But Layla was too much for him. Too abrupt. Too willing to try and rope him in. And she had literally just told him she did not have feelings for him. Why kiss him then? He flicked his glasses off his face and tossed them onto the dashboard. And why, in heaven's realm, did he wish for her to do it again?

∞

Rhea swiped a credit card and held the receipt down on the counter as the customer signed the slip. Chloe bagged the merchandise and smiled as she handed it over the counter. They high-fived when the person walked off and Rhea shot a thumbs up towards Layla across the shop as she mingled with more customers. "She may sell out tonight," Rhea whispered.

"Oh, I doubt that." Chloe motioned towards a small storage closet. "She's more in there if need be."

"That's good." Rhea's face split into a warm smile as Claron walked up and handed her a perfume bottle. She sniffed, and her eyes widened. "This is nice. And new."

"Layla says she made it for you. The smell of sunshine." Claron winked at her.

Rhea held a hand to her heart before spritzing and rubbing her wrists together. She wafted her arms around so Claron and Chloe could smell her.

"Well, what do you think?"

"'Tis lovely on you, Rhea," Chloe complimented.

Claron swooped in and kissed Rhea lightly on the neck. "Perhaps you should put some there too."

Rhea flushed and lightly nudged him away from her. "Perhaps I shouldn't wear this at all around you. It makes you crazy."

"Only crazy for you, love." He wriggled his eyebrows at her and she laughed. "Go away, you loon. I'm trying to be helpful."

Obliging, Claron grinned and walked towards his brothers Jaron and Tommy. Tommy stood holding a bag containing more shaving

cream. He didn't need any due to Layla providing him with some the week before, but true to O'Rifcan form, he was there to support Layla, and an additional bottle of cream was his way.

Layla beamed when her parents walked inside, her mam and da offering her loving embraces. Mr. O'Rifcan stood proudly, hands on his hips, as he looked about the room. "Quite possibly the most beautiful shop in County Clare," he boomed.

"Thank you, Da." Layla kissed his cheek. "I have refreshments on Chloe's counter if you'd like a glass of wine. Murphy and Piper be pouring for us." She motioned towards her brother and the friendly blonde from Galway as they argued behind Chloe's cashwrap.

"I think I will have a wee tipple." Claron Sr. walked towards his son and slapped a hand on the counter to interrupt the squabble between the two.

"Beautiful, love. Absolutely beautiful. And smells so lovely." Mrs. O'Rifcan slid an arm around Layla's waist. "And look how much you've sold. People from all over came here to shop. I'm so proud of you." She kissed Layla's cheek.

"Thanks, Mam." Layla looked down at her mammy and saw the tears puddling behind her eyes. "Oh, now don't start that, or I'll be a blubbering mess too."

"On with ye, then. A mammy is allowed to shed a tear when she's soon to burst of happiness. Now go." Sidna waved her off as she pulled a handkerchief from her pocket and dabbed her eyes. Riley walked up and slid his arm around her shoulders and pulled her into a hug. "We're all proud of our little brat tonight, Mammy. Very proud."

"Aye. She be a grand success."

Riley rubbed her back in soothing circles. Sidna looked up at him. "And where be your Heidi?"

"Layla has her restocking shelves." He pointed to his gorgeous girlfriend as she knelt in front of a display case and gingerly arranged several candles.

"So sweet of all the lasses to help her out tonight. Love seeing them all come together, being friends. Being family."

Riley beamed. "Aye. 'Tis still a wonder how Clary and I ended up with such brilliant women. Fairy work for certain."

"Bless'em," Sidna added and he laughed and gave her one final squeeze. "Enjoy yourself, Mam. All your ducklings are in a row."

"Aye. I believe I will, boyo." She kissed his cheek and released him and watched as he walked over

and extended a hand down to Heidi to help her to her feet.

Her boys were precious to her. All her children were. But to see them all so happy warmed her heart. She watched as Layla's eyes cast about the room and a brief disappointment settled over her features before she masked it and smiled at one of her customers. No doubt her daughter was looking for Delaney Hawkins. Mrs. O'Rifcan smiled to herself. Oh yes, she'd a mind to help that bud bloom. The reluctant man had no idea he was ensnared by her daughter. Or perhaps he did. But his unwillingness to accept it made Sidna proud. Layla needed a man who did not fall at her feet. For once, her daughter needed to be a part of the chase. She heard the bell above the door ring and Roland entered followed by Delaney, the two in deep conversation. Yes, he'd suit her daughter just fine. It was only a matter of time before Delaney would accept the fact that he'd lost his heart to her beautiful daughter. But she also felt it was her duty as mammy to nudge him along.

«CHAPTER ELEVEN»

Layla hurried over. Delaney looked up just in time to accept her excited embrace. She then hugged Roland in the same fashion. "I was wondering when you two would show up. I'm so glad you came." She linked her arm with Roland's. "I have just the potion for you, dear Roland."

"Is that so?" Rhea's grandpa straightened proudly at the attention as Layla escorted him towards a display of aftershaves and soaps. "A wee touch of peppermint is hidden in this." She held up a bar for him to smell.

"Peppermint, hm?" Roland's eyes sparkled as he reached into his vest pocket and retrieved a red

and white striped candy and handed it to her. She hastily unwrapped it and popped it into her mouth.

"Aye, peppermint." She kissed his cheek before moving onward towards Delaney. He stood chatting with Clary and Rhea. Layla smiled in greeting and reiterated. "'Tis about time you arrived... Delaney." She focused on Rhea. "Chloe manning the till?"

Rhea grinned sheepishly as she kissed Claron's cheek. "I was just headed back."

"You don't have to be so strict, Layla. They are helping you for free," Claron pointed out.

"I was just asking a question," Layla defended.

Claron tilted his head and squinted his eyes. "A question meant to incite obedience. What a great mammy you will be one day," he teased.

She playfully hit his shoulder. "If that's your way of calling me bossy, brother, I take offense."

"It is."

Biting back another retort, Layla turned her attention to Delaney. "And what can I interest you in today, Mr. Hawkins?" she asked, linking her arm with his. "Come for that cologne after all?"

"No. As previously discussed, Ms. O'Rifcan, I do not wear cologne."

She laughed and guided him towards the shelf that housed the familiar shower wash she'd once given him. "Then perhaps you need a replenishment." She handed him a larger bottle of the wash and smiled. When he looked at her, she exaggerated her charm by batting her lashes at him. He chuckled. "Is that how you upsell?"

"Aye. But it only works on me brothers, and possibly you."

He sighed. "I am a bit low on the bottle I have."

Her face gleamed in pleasure as he tucked the bottle under his arm and continued eyeing the space. "Thank you for coming, Delaney," she whispered, her blue eyes serious. "Tonight, as well as last night."

Uncomfortable with her gratitude, he shifted on his feet. "It was no trouble."

"Perhaps not, but it was kind, and I appreciate it nonetheless." She squeezed his hand. "I best make the rounds once more. Must continue those upsells." Her teeth flashed. "Promise you'll linger for a bit?"

"A bit," he agreed. She kissed his cheek in thanks, lingering just long enough for him to meet her eyes

once more and see her genuine appreciation before moving on towards Conor McCarthy's parents.

"You're a good sport." Riley walked up and handed him a glass of red wine.

Delaney nodded his thanks as he took a sip. "It's a nice set up. She's done well in creating a warm and inviting space."

"Aye. Layla's always had an eye for design. If she ever grew serious about it, I envision using her for some of my staging projects. But she's not one for leaving Castlebrook."

"That surprises me. She seems the adventurous type."

"To an extent. But her heart is here. Always has been." Riley took a sip of his own drink.

Layla hurried over to Riley. "Where be Conor, Riley? He was to finish my stools and people are wishing to sit."

Riley shrugged. "First off, you only asked for two stools, so I'm sure whichever two people wish for a seat can sit at the ones provided in Chloe's half of the shop for now. And Conor has been working on every O'Rifcan project under the sun. Give him a bit of slack, sister. The man's barely able to stand he's so worn out. I'm sure he'll be here in a bit."

Layla worried her bottom lip, her brow furrowed.

"Everyone is having a grand time, Layla," Delaney offered. "They do not expect to sit at tables and chat. They're here to buy your potions and mingle. Don't worry about seating."

Riley looked to Delaney in surprise for wishing to ease his sister's worry. "What Del said," Riley added.

"If you think so," she fretted.

"Besides, they're all going to end up at Murphy's Pub soon anyway. Again. 'Tis one of the reasons Piper came down from Galway to help out tonight."

"Oh Murphy..." Layla sighed as she watched her brother and Piper chat at the makeshift bar. She was in his debt for offering his services for the opening, and for free. No doubt Piper was volunteering as well. She was surrounded by help and service from her family and friends and she relaxed. "You buy Heidi more of her favorite salts?" she asked Riley.

"Aye. And lotion. And soap. And the candles to match. Oh, and the little potpourri bags for her drawers that she insisted she needed. A loyal customer, my Heidi."

"Good." Layla grinned.

"Well..." A female voice dripped in American roots, but polished with foreign flare carried over to them. Riley's smile widened as he opened his arm to accept a hug and two kisses to his cheeks as Rhea's Aunt Grace greeted the O'Rifcan siblings. "Such a lovely shop, Layla. Absolutely stunning. I brought some girlfriends with me and they adore your candles." She winked at the sister and then turned her eyes onto Delaney. "And who is this?" She extended her hand like royalty. Delaney awkwardly shook it instead of kissing it and Aunt Grace's lips twitched.

"This is Delaney Hawkins. This be Rhea and Heidi's boss in Limerick. And our friend," Riley added.

Acknowledgment flickered over her face. "Ah. Mr. Hawkins. So lovely to meet you. I'm Grace. I'm Rhea's aunt." Her perfectly painted lips smiled, and her blue eyes absorbed the handsome man before her. "I say, they must grow them right in Limerick."

Riley laughed as Delaney tried not to feel uncomfortable at her extra scrutiny. "Easy there, Grace, you're starting to make me feel like second fiddle."

Grace's laugh fluttered out as she playfully swatted Riley's arm. "Impossible, Riley dear. Absolutely impossible. Though I will admit I am intrigued. You know I love a man in a suit." She

winked at Riley as she linked her arm with Delaney's in friendly comradery.

"Best be careful, Grace. Layla's sight is set on this one and she can be a nasty green-eyed monster when need be."

Grace's brows rose, and she looked to Delaney. "Is that so? Well... I say, I'm pleased to see Layla has grabbed her a handsome one."

"I'm not—" Delaney started to interrupt but caught Riley's hard stare before continuing. He cleared his throat and fell silent.

"Oh look, there's Roland." She squeezed Delaney's arm before releasing him. "You two boys have fun, I'm going to go chat a spell." The men watched as she clicked her leopard print heels towards Roland and Claron Sr.

"She's an interesting woman," Delaney commented.

Riley chuckled. "Grace be a flirt with a heart of gold. Likes men of our age a bit more than her own."

"Ah." Delaney nodded in understanding. "Tread carefully then."

"Aye." Riley laughed. "Treading's been about all you've been doing lately, am I right?" Riley nodded towards his sister. Layla spotted them and gave a

brief wave before turning back to the women she spoke with.

"I don't know what you mean."

"Oh, come now, 'tis obvious Layla finds you of interest."

"I have no idea why."

Laughing harder, Riley slapped him on the back. "Aye, me either."

Somewhat offended, Delaney turned to him in surprise at his honesty.

"Only meaning I've never seen a man try so hard *not* to intrigue me sister. Typically, lads lay themselves at her feet. Nice to see one that doesn't."

"I have no intention for a relationship with Layla or anyone at the moment. Why would I engage in fruitless flirtation? Would that not just encourage it more? And then what? It would only hurt feelings in the long run."

"Unfortunately, Delaney," Riley turned to him with a tone of severity in his voice. "Layla has only deemed you a challenge. She's a determined one. Once she sets her mind to something or someone, she won't rest until she gets it. Best be prepared."

"The warning is noted. Perhaps I should leave then. I'd hate for her to get the wrong impression of my being here."

"No. You'll stay." Riley took a sip of his wine. "Because though you say you aren't comfortable with the thought of a flirtation, you also kind of like it. What man doesn't enjoy a beautiful woman chasing him down? Though I admit I was a bit scared when Heidi was on me tail." He chuckled. "But the best decision I ever made was for her to catch me. Wasn't in me plans or cards but turns out the fates had a better vision than I did. Don't underestimate her."

"Who? Fate or Layla?"

"Both." Riley winked at him as he held up his empty glass. "I think I'll go get a top off."

Delaney nodded in farewell as he brooded over Riley's words. It wasn't that he did not think Layla a beautiful and charming woman, of course she was. A bit abrasive at times, he'd admit. Though he factored that into part of her charm. Perhaps her attempts at kissing him or flirting with him were part of a game she liked playing, but he also remembered her crying in Rhea's office. That scene was forever engrained in his brain. There was more to the sister than she liked for others to see. And that's the part that intrigued him. He wanted to know the Layla underneath the sultry lashes and perfect smile. He just wasn't

quite sure how to go about it. Did he have to let her catch him before she displayed that side of herself? He hoped not. He'd much rather know every aspect of the woman before deciding whether or not he wished to date her. *Date?* He inwardly groaned at his line of thought. He was saved from further reflection when Claron walked up and extended him a hand to shake.

"I'm headed out, brother. Good of you to come." Clary shook his hand. "Early morning for me."

"Ah, of course, your cows."

Claron nodded. "Aye. They are the most punctual females I know, and our date comes bright and early."

"I could help you," Delaney offered.

Claron eyed him curiously.

"I mean, if it would be a help. I don't mind."

Claron smiled graciously. "I appreciate the offer, mate. But Rhea insists she is to be my help in the morning. She wishes to tend to the calves before I take them to me grands down in Cape Clear." Claron pointed to the door as Conor walked in hoisting two heavy stools. He set them beside Layla's counter. "That man definitely deserves a drink."

Layla hugged Conor in thanks as she ogled the stools in front of her. She rubbed her hand over the carvings and beamed.

"See to him, won't you?" Claron asked. "He be dead on his feet."

"I'll keep an eye out." Delaney offered.

"Good lad." Claron patted his shoulder as he walked towards an awaiting Rhea who offered a happy wave towards Delaney as they ducked out the door and walked up the sidewalk.

They started a trend and several people began to make their exit for the evening. Most headed towards Murphy's Pub as others drifted down the sidewalks or to their vehicles. Delaney hesitated a moment, not quite sure if he should head to the pub or home to Limerick. Murphy caught his eye and waved him over. "I need some hands, Delaney, would you mind?" He motioned towards a crate full of unopened wine bottles. "I'm packing it up to head to the pub. Seems I have customers already waiting."

Delaney set his glass on the counter and bent to lift the crate. He followed Murphy outside and towards the pub's entrance. Murphy was right, he had people lining the sidewalk waiting for the doors to open.

"Hold your appetites, mates," Murphy called to the people as he wound his way through the crowd with his own loaded crate. "Doors are opening. Give me a few minutes before demanding a drink. Need to get settled."

Piper rushed in behind them carrying her own crate full of empty glasses and ducked under the bar with them. She smiled at Delaney as he set his crate on the bar top. "You're a gem. Thanks." She took it and pulled it on her side of the bar.

"I'm to see Conor receives a drink," Delaney told Murphy.

"Aye. I'd give him a whole keg if I knew he could handle it." Murphy laughed. "I may offer him a bit of whiskey to start."

"As you should." Conor grinned as he slid onto a stool. Riley and Heidi stood behind him and Chloe sat next to him. She smiled at Delaney in greeting. "Make that two whiskeys brother. I be worn out as well," Chloe admitted.

"A successful round for all of us," Riley added.

"Aye. Give me a minute and I'll be back." Murphy finished putting away what he wished and as Piper expertly served one end of the bar, he set up the row of glasses for his family and one for himself. "To Layla's Potions," Chloe toasted, and everyone tossed back their first glass.

"Toasting without her... 'tis a shame. Perhaps we shall repeat the process when she comes in." Conor stated.

"And we will should she choose to," Chloe agreed. "She's tallying her receipts and taking inventory of her stock. She mentioned Clary's giant order of candles being her focus for the next week."

"There's no rush to that is there? He still hasn't settled on a date." Perplexed, Heidi looked up at Riley.

"Actually, he has," Chloe said. "Turns out when he called Rhea's da to ask his permission, Rhea's parents wished to fly out and witness the moment. Due to her da's work schedule, they can only come next weekend, otherwise it would be a good two months before they can travel. Clary doesn't wish to wait that long."

"Next week?!" Heidi threw up her hands. "And when did he plan on telling us all. We have an engagement party to plan."

Chloe laughed. "Aye, Layla's made a list and has started planning specifics as well as helping Clary fine tune his grand gesture."

"My part is easy enough," Conor said. "I just have to show up for the after party." He rubbed his hands together in anticipation.

"Should be a night that is not easily forgettable, that is for certain," Riley added. "I be rushing back from Galway for my part."

"I'm calling in sick that day," Heidi stated and then looked to Delaney and grimaced. "I mean, if that's okay? I was going to help Claron and Layla set the scene once he settled on the date."

"Quite fine. Take the day."

"But Rhea has to think I'm sick, not that I just took the day off. Remember that, Delaney."

"I won't forget." He tapped his temple.

"You'll come to the party, won't you, Delaney?" Chloe asked. "Would mean a lot to Rhea to have you there."

"Of course. Would love to." He stifled back a yawn. "Apologies." He tossed a few bills into the tip jar on the bar. "I think I will head on."

"I'd stop to say a farewell up the street if I were you," Riley quietly suggested.

Delaney nodded. "Night to you all."

"Night," the O'Rifcans resounded in unison.

Stuffing his hands into his pockets, Delaney headed up the sidewalk towards his car that was parked in front of Layla's shop. The lights were

dimmer as she sat on one of her new stools, head bent over a stack of receipts and a notebook. She clicked her fingers over a calculator and wrote something on the paper. She then tucked the pen into her hair which now rested in a sloppy bun on top of her head. There were several pens in her hair, and as he watched her read over something and then pat the counter looking for said pen, he smiled. She then reached into the holder across from her and plucked a new pen and the routine started again. He liked seeing the serious side of Layla. She was picturesque, as always, but a vulnerability radiated underneath the usual bravado. This was the Layla he wanted to get to know. And if Riley was correct, then Layla already wanted to know him better, despite what she'd said at her flat. Perhaps this was his opportunity to see the real Layla.

«CHAPTER TWELVE»

A tapping noise sounded on the glass door of the shop and had Layla looking up to find Delaney standing on the other side. Curious as to why he'd stopped back by, she stood and walked over to unlock the door. "You decide not to mingle at the pub already?"

"Was a bit tired," he explained. "Wanted to come by and say goodnight and congratulations." He motioned to the stack of receipts.

"'Twas a good night, indeed." She smiled and then held her hands to her cheeks. "I'm a bit overwhelmed at how wonderfully it went. Though I will admit I now feel a bit lost. Rhea set me up

with a bookkeeping system, but I'm having some trouble."

"Would you like me to help you?" he asked, motioning towards her notebook.

"Oh, no. I don't want to trouble you, Delaney. You're tired."

"I don't mind. If it helps point you in the right direction, it is best to start now than have to fix issues later."

"Spoken like a true accountant." She grinned. "I would be forever grateful if you could. Rhea told me it is best to work on paper and balance things out before entering them into the spreadsheet on the computer. But I can't seem to reach a balance."

"Let's take a look." Delaney walked over and sat on the opposite stool. Layla sat and watched as he gathered all her receipts from the night. He looked up at her and plucked a pen from her hair. She flinched a moment and then chuckled. "Ah, there they be." She then reached up and retrieved all her lost pens.

He pointed to the calculator and she handed it over. She watched as he expertly keyed in totals and flipped through the papers. His speed impressed her. When he'd finished that number, he wrote it in the notebook. He then counted the

till and wrote that number down. "And what was the starting amount in the till?"

She told him and he wrote it down. He then counted out the amount from what was there and handed the till tray back to her. "Your till is balanced. Now we must see if what is here in amounts matches the sales processed on your system." He then tallied the sums together and looked at her screen. He frowned. "It would appear you're a touch short. Any other receipts hiding about?"

She shook her head. "Not that I know of."

He stood and walked towards her cashwrap area and began lifting different things to check underneath them. He then pulled out the till drawer and tucked his hand behind it. "Ah." He pulled out a small white slip. "Fallen behind the till." He looked at the amount. "And it's for the very amount needed to reach your balance." He set it with the rest of the receipts. "And your total day's sales are..." He held up the calculator and Layla's eyes brightened. "That be what I made?!" She hopped to her feet on a squeal and clapped her hands. "That's amazing!"

"Now don't get too excited. You still have to factor in your cost of supplies and expenses. This just goes towards that."

"Aye, I know. But 'tis a fantastic start."

"That it is. Quite impressive." He set the calculator down. "Would you like me to check out the computer aspect that Rhea set you up with?"

"Well, perhaps you could watch me do it and make sure I'm doing it correctly? I do better by doing it."

He waved his hand towards her laptop. "Go ahead."

She pulled up a spreadsheet and began entering numbers in the correct columns. Rhea had done a thorough and extensive job helping Layla set up her bookkeeping. He was slightly proud of the fact it was his employee's skill that helped Layla now. She pressed enter and cheered. "They tally up just fine in here now too." She hit 'save' and then closed the laptop. "Thank you for helping me."

"My pleasure. I'm glad you had a successful night."

She sighed happily as she looked out over the sparse shelves and displays. "Aye. Now I plan to restock me shelves and then call it a night."

"You do not plan to celebrate over at Murphy's?" he asked, surprised that she wouldn't want to.

"Honestly, I'm quite buggered. I've been carrying around the weight of tonight for weeks and I think I will light some candles of me own and soak in a

luxurious bath with a glass of wine. Unwind. And fall asleep with a smile on my face."

"Sounds like a relaxing and indulgent evening." He stood. "I will not stand in your way. The sooner I leave, the sooner you will be finished."

"You could stay and keep me company." She walked over to her storage closet. "Only if you want." She turned before he could see the blush to her cheeks at asking him such a thing.

"I suppose I could help a bit longer."

Surprised, she bit back a smile before she turned. "Good. I'll have you set up some candles." She reached into the closet and pulled out a large box full of various scented candles. "Just place them on the shelf with the corresponding scent. I'll come behind and arrange them."

He nodded in understanding and did as he was asked. When he'd reached the last shelf, Layla walked over and fluffed the fresh lavender gracing the shelf and stagger stacked the candles amongst it. "There. All perfectly displayed." She caught him watching her and a newfound shyness washed over her. "What?"

Delaney blinked and shook his head. "Nothing. I just... it's neat to see this side of you."

"What side?"

"The serious side, I guess. Business oriented. Proud of your work."

"I am proud of it."

"As you should be. It's just... I haven't seen this side of you before."

She propped her elbow on the shelf and leaned her temple onto her fist. "Did you not think me capable?"

"No, that's not it," he added. "It's just a new side of you, Layla."

"Is it an appealing side, I hope?" Her uncertainty and vulnerability peeked through for a moment and had him smiling.

"Very much so," he admitted.

Her blue eyes danced a moment as she flushed at the praise. "Well, thank you, Delaney."

Silence hung between them as they stared at one another. Layla felt the slight change in his attention and braced herself for a kiss from the man she'd never thought would give her one.

Instead, Delaney cleared his throat and took a step back. "Well, I suppose my work here is done. I should go. I guess I will be seeing you again *next* weekend for the big proposal."

Disappointed, but pleased that Delaney seemed somewhat shaken by their recent interaction, Layla walked with him to the door. "Aye. 'Twill be a big celebration. Clary and Rhea." She shook her head and smiled. "She has absolutely no clue, and isn't that a grand thing?"

"I think so."

"Me too. 'Twill be fun pulling one over on her. Play your part, Delaney. No working late for her or you on Friday."

"I promise." He held up his hand in pledge.

"Good." She opened the door. "Safe travels back to Limerick."

He paused at the door and took a moment to gaze over her one more time. He reached up and plucked another pen from her hair. Embarrassed, Layla accepted it as he chuckled. "Night, Layla. Enjoy your night of well-earned indulgence." She shut the door on a contented sigh and nibbled her bottom lip as she wondered what a proposal from a man like Delaney might be like. Feeling fanciful, Layla tucked the pen in its proper holder and grabbed her purse, eager to meditate on that thought a bit more while lounging in her bubble bath.

∞

Delaney's phone rang again and he sighed. "Yes?"

"It's a Layla O'Rifcan for you, Mr. Hawkins. Again."

"Send her through." How was he to keep Rhea off their scent if Layla kept calling the office? "This is the fourth time you've called, Layla. It better be an emergency."

"Of course it is. Just making sure that Rhea is set to leave at five. We have most everything ready, but we will not be lighting the candles until we receive the call from Riley. Oh..." She paused as he heard her directing Chloe with the flowers. "Sorry about that. More decorations just arrived."

"I have given Rhea zero new projects so she should be out of the door at the right time."

"Fabulous. You're playing your part well, dear Delaney."

"I told you I would. Now, I would personally like to get some work done since I'm not playing hooky like Heidi or being specially treated by the boss like Rhea."

"Oh posh, you know you love being in the midst of our chaos." She giggled. "Don't forget to call me when she leaves. Wait, you don't have my number."

"I have it," Delaney replied.

"How's that? You've never asked me for it." The aggravation behind her words made him smile.

"You've called me four times today, remember? I'd be daft not to have written it down at some point."

"Oh." She murmured something to Claron and then heaved a heavy sigh. "I have to go, Delaney. Me poor brother is about to faint with nerves. You're a dear for helping with all this. Speak to you soon." She hung up and he placed his phone back in its cradle.

A knock sounded on his office door and Rhea poked her head inside his office. "Hey, so I'm pretty much twiddling my thumbs at the moment. Is there anything I can work on?"

"Ah..." Delaney paused.

Rhea waited patiently.

"You could see if there's anything you could help Heidi with. Since she's out today you might see what she has almost finished up."

"Great." Rhea smiled and turned to leave but pivoted at the door and cast him a surveying glance. "You alright today?"

He nodded. "Why?"

"You just seem... distracted."

"Oh, well... just wrapping up the busy season has me thinking about a vacation, I guess."

"I hear ya. Will be nice once things slow down a bit. Seems like we've had a hectic month. Will be nice to have a breather soon."

Knowing Rhea was about to have an even more hectic evening and weekend had him trying to keep a straight face. "Yes. It will."

"Oh, so how's it been going with Layla?" she asked. "I haven't really had a chance to talk to you about it since... well, that day at the elevators. I wasn't sure if you guys were still interested in one another or what?"

Delaney wasn't sure what to say. Cornered, he fidgeted in his chair.

"Sorry, none of my business." She held up her hands in defeat. "I was just curious." She smiled. "I'll go check Heidi's files now." She exited and Delaney exhaled in relief. He eyed the stack of files on his desk and pulled the next one off the top. He only had an hour before it was time to leave. Perhaps by then he'd be able to relax. But as the phone rang again, he grumbled as he answered.

∞

"No, no, no." Layla called and rushed towards Jace. "The arch is to stay where it is at. I asked you to move the pillar." She pointed to the wooden scrolled stump. "Just a wee bit to the left. Jace obliged and then stepped back. Layla nodded in approval. "Chloe, flowers can come for the pillar now." Layla took a step back and eyed the beautiful set up. Her Mammy and Mrs. McCarthy had been working on a feast all day for the engagement party, and Layla had just finished the location. Several round tables boasted full table settings, luscious bouquets, and overflowing vases of flowers courtesy of her sister. Checking off on her mental list, Layla then turned towards the house. She walked in and Clary stood with his hands braced upon the table top looking down at Riley's drafts of the cottage. "What if she hates it?" he asked, looking up at her.

Layla shook her head. "Stop second guessing yourself, brother. Rhea will love it. Leave it be and go take a shower to freshen up. You have less than two hours and you will be an engaged man.

"You've got the candles?"

"Aye, I will have it all set up."

"Don't set them too close to the drafts, I don't want wax to drip on them."

"I won't, Clary. Stop your worry. It will be beautiful. Now go. Shower. Clean up. And then go to where you will be in position."

"And you have the video ready?"

"Yes."

"And her parents. Roland has them?"

"Aye. Roland checked in an hour ago and had them at his flat. Everyone is ready."

"And Riley? He is ready?"

"Clary!" Layla gripped his shoulders and shook him. "Everything is going as planned. Relax." She chuckled as his worried gaze drifted over his house. "Go." She turned him towards his room.

Confident he'd found his way, finally, she went about rearranging his dining area. She loved that he had a round table and the drafts centered there and the candles would be lit in an arch around them. Chloe had placed flower garlands draped around the curtains and across the window sills, petals would eventually line the walkway from the garden gate to the door for Rhea to follow. Layla would be hidden in the living room so as to record the proposal and Rhea's reaction. All would be set. She looked at her watch. She bustled out the door and spotted Chloe placing a flower arrangement on the stump pillar Jace had

just placed. The flowers billowed down the sides and looked phenomenal and whimsical. Her family had come together for what would be a magical night. Rhea was going to faint. Smiling, she glanced at her watch again. She should be hearing from Riley by now. She dialed his number.

"I'm trying." His first response had her back stiffen.

"What do you mean you're trying, brother?"

"Got a bit delayed in a meeting. I'm headed back to me office now to grab me truck and will be headed that way."

"You haven't even left Galway yet?!" Layla tried to tamper down her temper and her voice. "Riley O'Rifcan, this be Clary's biggest night, you will not screw it up."

"I know. I know. I'm hurrying. See if you can buy me like twenty minutes, yeah?"

Growling, Layla hung up. She felt a slight sense of panic when Claron walked out of the cottage door looking fresh and handsome. He'd changed into a pale blue button up shirt, the sleeves rolled partially up his arms, and his best pair of denims. She smiled proudly.

"We hear from Riley?" he asked.

"Aye. Just spoke to him."

"And he's ready?"

"Aye," she lied. "Perfectly in place."

"Good." Claron rubbed his hands together nervously. "And Roland?"

"Was just about to call him."

"Good. I'm going to check out the dinner tables." He wandered off and she heaved a sigh and dialed Roland's number.

"Layla dear, we are ready."

"So good to hear Roland. Now, just a refresher, you are to meet Rhea at the gate."

"Yes. I remember."

"And Jeanie and Paul are to be waiting with the others at the barns. No cars in sight."

"Yes. Murphy has already directed us where to park."

"Good. See you in a bit." She hung up and flashed a quick eye to her watch. Time was ticking. How could she get Riley those extra minutes?

«CHAPTER THIRTEEN»

Delaney rode the elevator in silence as Rhea looked at her phone with a worried expression.

"Something wrong, Rhea?"

"I just haven't heard from Claron today. Normally he texts me throughout the day. I hope something isn't wrong."

"I'm sure everything is fine. He's probably just in the midst of milking."

"That's not until six," she replied without glancing up and dialed Claron's number again. Voicemail. The elevator doors swished open and they walked

towards the parking lot. She paused as she went to unlock her car. "Seriously?"

"What's that?" Delaney called from his car.

"I have a punctured tire." She pointed, and Delaney walked around to check. Sure enough, Rhea's rear wheel was completely flattened. Thoughts of Layla's schedule and time frame for Rhea crossed his mind.

"I need to call a service," Rhea said and began searching in her phone for a number to call.

"Why don't I give you a ride?" Delaney said. "We can leave your car here and have Riley retrieve it when he's back in town tomorrow."

"I don't want you to have to drive out of your way."

"It's not." He tampered down the slight urgency in his voice. "I, um... planned to visit Layla this evening, so I was headed to Castlebrook anyway." Not exactly a lie, he told himself.

"Oh." Hope lit Rhea's face. "Then that would be great. Let me call Riley and let him know."

Delaney nodded as he opened his passenger door and Rhea slid inside with the phone at her ear. He heard her report the situation to Riley and her current offer from Delaney. He grabbed his own phone and texted Layla about their change in plans. Seems he would be bringing

Rhea to her proposal tonight. Not entirely what he had planned, but he was bound to roll with the punches.

Layla quickly responded that he was to drop Rhea off at O'Brien's Bridge to Riley. Under no circumstances was he to drive her all the way to Clary's. For Riley had a part to play in the proposal plan. Delaney agreed to her terms and received a kissy face in response.

Rhea hung up and sighed. "Thanks for this, Delaney. I don't know what it is about Ireland, but I've had more flat tires here than I ever did back in Maryland."

"Just a bump in the road. They're a nuisance to be sure. But glad I could help."

"I'm headed straight to Claron's, if you don't mind. We plan to have a meal with my grandpa tonight."

"That sounds lovely."

Rhea's worry lessened, and she smiled. "Yes, it will be. Claron's been good to Grandpa. A friend. They have a special relationship. I'm glad I found a man who appreciates him."

Delaney drove a bit slower than the traffic surrounding them and he prayed Rhea did not notice or mention it. But Layla had asked him to drag out the drive a bit to give Riley a bit more

time to reach his position. Another car passed them, and he spotted Rhea take a quick glance at her watch. He tried not to smile. She was too polite to say anything, he realized, and he continued to coast along.

"Is this the way you always take?" Rhea asked.

"Pardon?"

"Well, it's just that O'Brien's Bridge is a bit out of the way."

"Oh, right. I enjoy the scenic route on a Friday. Helps relax me after a long week. The river is beautiful coming into Castlebrook that way."

"I see." Rhea smirked.

"What's that look?"

Rhea laughed. "Delaney, don't take this the wrong way, but you're kind of a nerd."

Baffled at her bravery, he gawked before straightening in his seat. "I am not. Enjoying a pretty view on my drive is not unheard of. Plenty of people do it."

"Right. While listening to Mozart? While driving twenty kilometers under the speed limit?" Rhea giggled. "It's charming, don't get me wrong. It just makes me laugh."

Unoffended, Delaney grinned. "I guess I am a bit of a 'nerd' as you say."

As he made the turn onto the road leading to the bridge, a truck sat to the side and a head of dark hair stood next to it. Rhea squinted. "Is that Riley?"

Relieved, Delaney pulled his car over and slowly parked behind the O'Rifcan brother. Rhea looked to him in confusion. "I am handing you off now, Rhea."

Her brow furrowed. "I don't understand."

"He offered to meet me here, so I could immediately head to Layla."

"Oh. Well, thank you for bringing me this far. I appreciate it."

"No problem." Delaney smiled and opened his mouth to say something else but closed it so as not to tip Rhea off. "Have a good night, Rhea."

"Thanks." She stepped out and Riley walked towards her. He offered a wave to Delaney. And so as not to overshadow his words with the sound of his car, Delaney waited a moment. He cracked his window a bit to listen.

"Rhea darling." Riley grinned.

"Thanks for meeting Delaney. I hate having to bum rides off people."

Riley flicked a rose from behind his back and Rhea eyed him suspiciously. "And what's that?"

"'Tis a rose, dear Rhea." He laughed. "For you."

"That's sweet. But why are you greeting me with a rose when your girlfriend is at home sick?"

He chuckled as he opened the door to his truck. "It's only right for me to pick you up here. 'Tis where I found you on your first day in Ireland, love."

Still confused, Rhea just shook her head and climbed into his truck. "Okay. Well, thank you for the rose."

"'Tis just the first rose of the night, Rhea darling."

She turned to him. "What? Why?"

"Let's just say Clary is wanting to spoil you tonight."

"Oh, that's sweet. Well, he better. He didn't text me at all today. I thought something might be wro—" Her eyes widened. "Wait."

Riley's smile only grew as he cranked his engine.

Delaney could hear Rhea's excited squeals as Riley pulled away from the side of the road and

headed towards Castlebrook. He quickly texted Layla they were on the move.

∞

"Alright, people!" Layla called. "Clary, in your spot. Roland, at the gate. Everyone else to the barns until I text. Hurry, hurry, hurry." She smiled as Rhea's excited mother linked her arm with Murphy's and allowed her handsome brother to escort her across the grass. Everyone hustled and Rhea's father, Paul, lingered a moment longer. He extended his hand to Claron. "Take a deep breath, son." He chuckled as Claron did as he suggested. He gave a friendly pat to Claron's shoulder. "Thankful for you. Can't wait to see my Rhea even happier than you've already made her."

"Thank you, Mr. Conners."

"It's Paul."

"Paul." Claron's nervous smile had the man giving him an extra pat before following the others.

"I'm inside, Clary. Hiding. Video ready. Candles lit. Good luck, brother." Layla kissed him on the cheek as she hurried inside. She quickly lit the candles surrounding the architectural drafts of Claron's house and then scattered a few extra flower petals across the floor before finding her spot behind the leather chair. She made sure her camera was propped properly and ready to go and then took a

deep breath. "Showtime," she whispered as she heard a car pull into the drive.

She heard Claron crack the door. "She's here."

"I'm ready," Layla called softly. She heard Roland's voice.

"About time you two arrived." Roland beamed as he extended a rose towards Rhea. She looked from Roland to Riley and both smiled at her.

"When you first came to Castlebrook, I found you at O'Brien's Bridge and it was my duty to deliver you to Roland. I am to fulfill that duty again tonight." Riley bent down and kissed Rhea's cheek before nudging her forward.

Roland opened the small white gate that led to the path leading to Claron's door. Claron stood on the stoop, but he didn't move, and Rhea tried not to rush the excitement that filled her heart. She noticed the path was covered in flower petals and a tear escaped and slid down her cheek. Roland patted her hand as he escorted her towards Claron.

"When you arrived at Sidna's B&B to see me, I wasn't there. I was late... out fishing like I do." He felt her hand grip his in nervous jitters and he grinned. "But in that moment of my tardiness, you met another O'Rifcan brother. And he is the one that saw to you for that first family meal." He

stopped at the stoop and rested her hand in Claron's. "And it is my pleasure and honor that I am able to see that he will forever make you feel welcome at the family meal." Roland choked on his last words which made Rhea begin to cry as she embraced him. She then turned to Claron as he took both her hands, her rose stems squishing between their fingers. Roland exited quietly, and Layla heard Clary's voice drift through the door.

"Rhea love," He smiled nervously, and she tried to stifle her tears. He chuckled. "You're supposed to save those for later."

"I can't help it. I'm sorry." She laughed behind the tears.

"No need to say sorry, love." He gently wiped away a few of her tears. "Rhea, from the moment I saw you standing on the stairs at Mam's, I wanted you to be mine."

She sniffled.

"As I grew to know you, I knew deep down that we were meant."

She sniffled as he opened his door and began leading her inside.

"The first time you helped me at the dairy I knew I would never be able to picture myself here without you."

As they stepped into the house, Layla focused the camera on them and Rhea's eyes widened as she surveyed the candles and flowers.

"Now that I have you, my only wish now is to make it be forever. However long that may be, Rhea love, I wish for you to be by my side." He motioned towards the plans on his table. "I want to build a future with you. Love you. Build a family with you. Create a loving home." He motioned to the expansion of the cottage and Rhea gasped, her hands covering her mouth as she walked closer to the table and looked over the drawings, Claron standing behind her and watching. He knelt to his knee and waited.

"Claron, this is—" She turned around and gasped again while stifling an excited giggle. He grinned as he held up the ring.

"Your Roland gave me this ring," he explained. "Belonged to your grandmother."

Rhea eyed the ring in wonder.

"I thought it was quite fitting for me to give to you. A symbol, so to speak, of your family merging with mine. To forever be on your finger as my wife and my beloved, while also representing the history of devotion from your own family."

"It's beautiful," Rhea whispered.

"So, Rhea darling," he began and Rhea's face split into an enormous smile. "Will you do me the honor of—"

"Yes!" she squealed, slightly hopping in place. "I'm sorry... I mean... finish. Go on. Finish what you were going to ask."

Claron laughed. "Will you be me wife?"

"Yes!" She replied again with the same vigor. He slipped the ring onto her finger and she briefly looked at it before lunging into his arms and wrapping them around his neck.

Layla gave them a moment as they kissed and whispered promises to one another before turning off the camera. She texted Murphy to tell the others to come to the party area.

Claron eased her back and kissed her one last time before heading towards the door. "Come with me, love."

"What else could there possibly be?" She excitedly let him drag her down the stairs and she paused.

"Mom?" Shock had Rhea freezing in place as Jeanie Conners stood on the other side of the garden fence and waited to embrace her daughter. "Mom!" Rhea ran to her and enveloped her in a tight hug. "I can't believe you're here." She looked at Claron

and linked her hand with his. "I can't believe all of this."

"It's not over yet, honey." Jeanie opened the gate and motioned towards the edge of the cliff where the tables were set up. Rhea's jaw dropped as she saw all those she loved. As they made their way forward, cheers erupted and everyone they passed by hugged and congratulated them. Rhea floated from one person to the next in complete awe at what Clary had done for her.

∞

Delaney waited by the cottage as he saw the flickers of candle flames slowly be blown out. Layla slipped out the door to head towards the celebration.

"Another wondrous night you've planned, Layla."

His voice had her jumping, her hand on her heart.

"You scared me." She walked forward and linked her arm with his as they began to walk towards he crowd. "It was beautiful."

He could tell she'd been crying and did not shy away when she gently rested her head on his shoulder as they walked. "I'm so happy for the two of them. He was so nervous."

"Any man would be."

Rhea spotted them and ran towards Layla and almost knocked her over when she wrapped her in a tight hug. She then held out her hand. "Can you believe it?"

"'Tis beautiful, Rhea love. Absolutely gorgeous."

"Thank you." Rhea held Layla's hands and cried as she spoke. "For helping him put all this together."

"Oh now, what makes you think I had anything to do with it?"

"The candles. They were my scent. Pure sunshine."

Layla held her tongue in cheek at being discovered and Rhea pulled her into another hug. "Thank you, Layla. I love you and am so excited to be your sister."

"Oh now, posh, here they come again." Layla began to cry as well and squeezed Rhea tight before nudging her back towards her awaiting brother. "On with ye, Rhea. Enjoy your night."

Delaney handed her a napkin and she dabbed under her eyes. "The trick is to catch them," she said.

"Catch what?"

"The tears." She sniffled and looked towards the setting sun with wide eyes so as to dry them in the light breeze. "Did my mascara run?" she asked him.

He looked her over. "No."

"Good." She smiled. "Come, let's celebrate."

Delaney stepped forward and Roland introduced him to Rhea's parents. Rhea mirrored her mother almost perfectly minus a few fine lines, and Jeanie Conners was just as emotional at her daughter's proposal as the other women Delaney encountered. He accepted the intense embrace from Mrs. O'Rifcan and politely avoided her suggestions for him to be by Layla's side the entire time. Though he did find himself drawn to Layla as she shared in the festivities. He caught her eye and was grateful for the interruption from Mrs. O'Rifcan as Layla waved him over. He excused himself and made his way towards Layla and Chloe.

"Saved you." Layla elbowed him playfully in the side and he flushed at being so transparent.

Chloe laughed. "Mammy has a way of chatting the ears off anyone."

"She does love to talk," Layla added.

"A bit," Delaney admitted.

Heidi walked by with two glasses and winked at Delaney in passing as she made her way towards Riley, who was speaking to Rhea's father.

Conor walked up and handed Layla and Chloe each a glass of wine. "Sorry there, Delaney, I only grabbed the girls one."

"Not to worry, Conor. I was just on my way that direction." He started to walk away, and Layla grabbed his hand.

"Can I come?" she asked.

Looking down at their joined hands, he nodded. "Sure."

A bright smile swept over her face as they walked towards the drink table and he poured himself a glass.

As the sun continued setting over Angel's Gap, twinkle lights and candles provided the much needed light for everyone to help themselves to the delicious spread provided by Sidna and Mrs. McCarthy.

Delaney watched as Rhea continued to shake her head in awe at the elaborate plan that continued to develop before her. Her eyes shined when she looked at Claron, and the man was equally enraptured with her. Delaney felt a tug in his chest at the sight of them together. *What must it be like to share that kind of love with someone*, he wondered. His parents weren't quite the example of love in a marriage. He'd watched for years how his mother suffered from lack of affection from his

father, and how his father occupied himself with work instead of family. Delaney was determined that when his time came, he'd love wholeheartedly. But perhaps that was his problem. He'd been waiting and putting it off so long because he feared he'd fail. He feared he'd be trapped in a loveless marriage like his parents. Had he turned into his father without realizing it? Did he occupy himself with work so as to avoid disappointing a spouse or himself?

Looking around at the O'Rifcan family he only felt a sense of longing. Close-knit togetherness he never would have fathomed if it had not been for him meeting Rhea and watching her journey with them. He jolted at the slap on the back and immediately knew Riley had walked up to chat. Even that annoying habit didn't seem so bothersome now.

"Glad you came to the rescue tonight, Del. Rhea told me of your slow driving and 'scenic route.'" He laughed. "Bought me the minutes I needed."

"Glad I could help." He shook Riley's hand. "And... thank you."

"For what?" Riley asked.

"Last weekend. For telling me to stop by Layla's shop on my way out. I was able to see a side of her I hadn't seen yet."

"And?"

Delaney tilted his head. "And I'm not sure yet."

"Well that's better than where you were at before, so I will gladly take the credit." Riley chuckled as he nodded towards Layla as she helped clear some of the dishes into a large basket, her mother pointing out various settings that needed tending. "Perhaps you can rescue her from dish duty. Our Layla has served well today helping put all this together."

"Right. I might just do that." Delaney straightened his tie and began walking Layla's direction.

∞

"Might I steal you away?"

Layla looked up to see Delaney, hands in pockets, leaning over the table to murmur to her. She looked down at the basket of dishes and towards her mam at the other end of the table.

"You could carry this heavy basket to me da's truck and then I will allow you to whisk me away."

"I could do that." He reached for the basket and his hands brushed hers. Surprise lit her gaze as he didn't pull away as he normally would. She released the handles and nodded for him to follow her. When he set the basket in the back of an

ancient green vehicle, he turned to her expectantly.

"And where might you be taking me, Delaney?"

He shrugged nervously and nudged his glasses up his nose which made her smile. "Honestly, I hadn't quite thought that far ahead."

Intrigued, Layla reached for his hand. "Come then. I'll show you the best spot on Angel's Gap." She led him towards the cliff, the sound of the River Shannon billowing beneath them. "Rhea will be quite spoiled now, waking up to this." Layla motioned before them as Delaney eyed the steep drop off and beautiful spread below them. The sun began to stoop behind the skyline and dusk settled around them as comfortable as one of her mammy's knitted blankets.

"It's a beautiful spot. They will be happy here."

"Aye. I believe they will." She squeezed his hand. "Are you worried she will quit her job in Limerick?"

"I've been worried about that since the first time I saw them together," he admitted.

"Perhaps you could create a new position for her."

"And what would that be?"

"Would she really need to be in the office every day?" Layla asked.

"I suppose not."

"And could she not work from home?" She waved her hand towards the cottage.

"Possibly so."

"And—"

"Okay enough." Delaney chuckled as Layla grinned. "Rhea has yet to even think about quitting. I don't want to cross that bridge until it comes."

"One step at a time."

"Exactly."

"Well, would your steps be finding their way to Castlebrook next weekend?"

Delaney heaved an exaggerated sigh. "That would be five weekends in a row for me. Seems a bit much."

"What if it were for a grand reason?" Layla laced her fingers with his and hugged their arms close.

"And what reason would that be?" He asked, looking down into her beaming face.

"Me."

His brows rose and he saw the brief uncertainty she held at being so bold towards him. "Sounds like a justifiable reason."

She elbowed him in the ribs and he grunted. "You're a mystery, Mr. Hawkins."

"Are we back to that now? And here I thought we had turned a page."

"Have we?" she asked, gently tugging on his tie.

"Easy now, I'm new to this."

She laughed. "And I'm not. Does that bother you?"

"No."

"So sure." Impressed, she leaned back and looked up at him. "I don't quite know how to respond."

"You could let it be. Take it one step at a time." He grinned at using her own words against her.

"Aye, I think I could do that." The doubt his expression held had her bursting into laughter. "I will try my best," she amended. "But could you at least do one thing for me, Delaney?"

"And what would that be?"

"Would you bloody kiss me already?"

A sarcastic retort about waiting for such a step in their relationship froze on his lips as Layla pressed

her mouth to his. Only this time, he took tender care of kissing her in return. A kiss of promise, uncertainty, and a touch of faith, that gave Delaney hope for the future and melted Layla's heart.

Continue the story with...

Book Four of
The Siblings O'Rifcan Series

All Books in
The Siblings O'Rifcan Series:
Claron
Riley
Layla
Chloe
Murphy

All titles by Katharine E. Hamilton
Available on Amazon and Amazon Kindle

Adult Fiction:

The Unfading Lands Series
The Unfading Lands, Part One
Darkness Divided, Part Two
Redemption Rising, Part Three

The Lighthearted Collection
Chicago's Best
Montgomery House
Beautiful Fury

Children's Literature:
The Adventurous Life of Laura Bell
Susie At Your Service
Sissy and Kat

Short Stories:
If the Shoe Fits

Find out more about Katharine and her works at:
www.katharinehamilton.com

Social Media is a great way to connect with Katharine. Check her out on the following:

Facebook: Katharine E. Hamilton
https://www.facebook.com/Katharine-E-Hamilton-282475125097433/

Twitter: @AuthorKatharine
Instagram: @AuthorKatharine

Contact Katharine:
khamiltonauthor@gmail.com

ABOUT THE AUTHOR

Katharine E. Hamilton began writing a decade ago by introducing children to three fun stories based on family and friends in her own life. Though she enjoyed writing for children, Katharine moved into adult fiction in 2015 with the release of her first novel, The Unfading Lands, a clean, epic fantasy that landed in Amazon's Hot 100 New Releases on its fourth day of publication and reached #72 in the Top 100 Bestsellers on all of Amazon in its first week. The series did not stop there and the following two books in The Unfading Lands series released in late 2015 and early 2016.

Though comfortable in the fantasy genre, Katharine decided to venture into romance in 2017 and released the first novel in a collection of sweet, clean romances: The Lighthearted Collection. The collection's works would go on to reach bestseller statuses and win Reader's Choice Awards and various Indie Book Awards in 2017 and early 2018.

Katharine has contributed to charitable Indie anthologies and helped other aspiring writers journey their way through the publication process. She loves everything to do with writing and loves that she can continue to share heartwarming stories to a wide array of readers.

She was born and raised in the state of Texas, where she currently resides on a ranch in the heart of brush country with her husband, Brad, and their son, Everett, and their two furry friends, Tulip and Cash. She is a graduate of Texas A&M University, where she received a Bachelor's degree in History.

She is thankful to her readers for allowing her the privilege to turn her dreams into a new adventure for us all.

D1497608

CPSIA information can be obtained
at www.ICGtesting.com
Printed in the USA
LVHW100754020622
720261LV00002B/275

9 780692 192627